BABY ON BOARD

From bump to baby and beyond…

Whether she's expecting or they're adopting—
a special arrival is on its way!

Follow the tears and triumphs
as these couples find their lives
blessed with the magic of parenthood….

**Baby on Board goes Down Under
in the special Outback Baby Tales trilogy.**

Available April 2010

One Small Miracle
by Melissa James

Available May 2010

The Cattleman, the Baby and Me
by Michelle Douglas

Available June 2010

Their Newborn Gift
by Nikki Logan

Dear Reader,

Family is such a big part of my life, and I take joy in bringing that closeness to the characters in my stories. My new nephew is so good with his baby girl; I love to watch them together. Nothing is more touching than a strong man holding a defenseless baby with gentle devotion.

In *Sheriff Needs a Nanny* a man of moral and physical strength struggles to find the emotional depth to connect with his baby boy when he's forced to take on the boy's care. Luckily the nanny he hires knows just what father and son need to bring them together. I wish you joy in their journey.

Teresa Carpenter

www.teresacarpenter.net

TERESA CARPENTER

Sheriff Needs a Nanny

TORONTO • NEW YORK • LONDON
AMSTERDAM • PARIS • SYDNEY • HAMBURG
STOCKHOLM • ATHENS • TOKYO • MILAN • MADRID
PRAGUE • WARSAW • BUDAPEST • AUCKLAND

Recycling programs
for this product may
not exist in your area.

ISBN-13: 978-0-373-17645-8

SHERIFF NEEDS A NANNY

First North American Publication 2010.

Copyright © 2010 by Teresa Carpenter.

www.eHarlequin.com

Printed in U.S.A.

Teresa Carpenter believes in the power of unconditional love and that there's no better place to find it than between the pages of a romance novel. Reading is a passion for Teresa—a passion that led to a calling. She began writing more than twenty years ago, and marks the sale of her first book as one of her happiest memories. Teresa gives back to her craft by volunteering her time to Romance Writers of America on a local and national level. A fifth generation Californian, she lives in San Diego within miles of her extensive family and knows with their help she can accomplish anything. She takes particular joy and pride in her nieces and nephews, who are all bright, fit, shining stars of the future. If she's not at a family event you'll usually find her at home reading, writing or playing with her adopted Chihuahua, Jefe.

"Teresa Carpenter's *Her Baby, His Proposal* makes an oft-used premise work brilliantly through skilled plotting, deft characterization and just the right amount of humor."

—*RT Book Reviews*

For Mom, who has always believed in me.
And for Yvonne, JD, Denise and all the Culversons
for their loving care of Mom this last year.
You guys are the best. And for Rodney
and Brandon, daddies extraordinaire!

CHAPTER ONE

"HERE goes everything." Nicole Rhodes arrived at the front door of the sprawling ranch-style house. She glanced down at her navy ruffled vest, white tank and tailored khaki Capris. Together with her white sandals she felt she'd hit the right mark of cool and professional.

Two adjectives she rarely aspired to. She preferred to experience life.

Still, for today, going on her first job interview in five years, she needed all the confidence she could muster. Damn state budget cuts. She was one of a thousand teachers looking for alternative employment.

Pasting a smile on her face, she knocked on the door.

She needed a job and a place to stay ASAP. This nanny position offered both, with the added bonus of allowing her to stay close to her very pregnant sister, Amanda.

The door in front of her opened to frame a half-naked man. *Oh, mama.*

Her internal temperature spiked to match the hundred-degree heat as she admired six-pack abs, a strong chest dusted with dark hair attached to a corded neck, and a head buried in a gray cotton T-shirt.

"Hey, Russ." A deep voice came from within the depths of bunched-up material. "Thanks for coming over so quickly. I've been picking up before the nanny gets here. I've only got ten minutes to grab a quick shower."

Before she could respond, the shirt finished its journey, leaving mussed mink-brown hair in its wake. A myriad of emotions flowed over Sheriff Trace Oliver's sharp-edged features. Surprise, annoyance and finally resignation flashed through eyes the color of lush green grass.

"I suppose it's too much to hope you're Russ's older sister, come to help out in a crunch?"

She shook her head, felt the heavy weight of the long brunette mane hanging down her back and vaguely wished she'd pulled it up and off her neck. Smiling, and doing her best to ignore all the toned, tanned skin on display, she held out a hand.

"Nikki Rhodes, potential nanny," she introduced herself.

"You're early." The words were curt as he gripped her hand and let his intense gaze roam over her. Ever the optimist, she decided to take his comment as an observation rather than an admonishment.

"Yes. It's supposed to be an admirable trait."

In sheer self-preservation she broke away from his forceful gaze. Instead her glance fell to where her hand lay, cradled in his warm, strong grasp.

"Not always." He responded to her comment with a grimace, and motioned to his shorts and bare chest.

Oh, man. And she'd been trying so hard not to stare. She didn't want to think of her charge's father in a physical way. It just made for unwanted complications. She cleared her throat.

"I'll remember that for the future." She nodded her head toward her silver Camry at the curb. "Shall I wait in the car while you shower?"

"What? No." He stepped back, drawing her inside. "Please come in." He frowned at their clasped hands, as if surprised to find her hand still in his. Abruptly, he released her. "I'll adjust."

Nikki followed him inside; she took in the living room, small dining-room-kitchen combo, and wondered what he could possibly have had to pick up in anticipation of her visit. The rooms were buffed to a high gloss and lacked any form of clutter. The furniture, what there was of it, was all large and modern, all straight lines and muted blues and grays. Nothing in the room suggested a baby lived there. In fact, it had a military feel to it.

One glance around the everything-in-its-place interior and she recognized his need for control. Oh, yeah, she'd been there, lived with that and had no desire to repeat the experience. Reason number two why she should end this interview now.

Amanda, at home on bedrest, kept Nikki's feet planted right where she stood.

"Have a seat," he said. "I'm going to grab a clean shirt."

Yes, please. Cover up all that gorgeous toned skin.

"Girl, you are in so much trouble," she muttered under her breath, watching him disappear down a short hall.

She had no business noticing a prospective employer in that way. It said so right in her contract with the agency.

And she needed this job. She'd given up her apartment three months ago, and moved in with her sister while her brother-in-law was out to sea. Her intent was to save for a down payment on a condo. The timing had seemed perfect. Nikki would keep her sister company and help her to get ready for her first baby, then Nikki would move into her own place just before hubby and baby were due to arrive.

Instead Nikki had received a pink slip. And her brother-in-law had returned two weeks early. Yeah, perfect timing. She was very much the squeaky third wheel in the tiny two-bedroom house, but Amanda wouldn't hear about Nikki moving until she had a new job.

She had good credentials, so she didn't worry about being employable, but this was the only gig in Paradise Pines, and it was important to her that she stay close to her sister until she had the baby.

But Nikki's reluctance to walk away was about more than that. Since the day she'd left for college, and discovered a sense of freedom she'd never known at home, she'd vowed to live life—not hide from it.

Still, she needed to protect herself. She tended to give her heart easily. It was one of the reasons she'd chosen to work with young children. They thrived on her affection and were honest in their responses. She could trust them with her soft heart.

Sheriff Oliver didn't look as if he knew the definition of soft. He was all about neatness, control and schedules. She'd bet structure and discipline were two of his favorite words. Babies were messy, chaotic and unpredictable. Discipline and structure were important, but so was flexibility and creativity. A baby needed room to grow, to makes mistakes and messes in order to learn.

If she took this job, Nikki saw nothing but strife and loggerheads ahead, because she would fight for what was best for the baby. Maybe even harder than she needed to, because the situation hit so close to home.

When Sheriff Oliver returned, he wore blue jeans and a dark green shirt that did incredible things for his eyes. Eyes cooler now than when he'd left the room. As were his features.

He'd gathered his guard, something he wore with such ease she knew it was what he usually showed the world. They'd only stumbled into that moment of rare unease because she'd surprised him at the door.

"The agency said you're a kindergarten teacher," he said as he sat in the recliner adjacent to the couch she occupied. "You know this is a live-in position?"

Down to business. Good. Maybe they'd make it through this interview yet.

"Yes. I'm a victim of the recent state budget cuts." She gave a jaunty shrug, pretending to him—and herself—that losing her job was just a blip in life's journey. "But I was a nanny before; it helped pay my way through college."

"You juggled kids and school? Quite a feat. Most mothers don't even attempt it."

"I had the kids during the day, so I took most of my classes at night. The Hendersons knew I was in school, so they respected my hours. It worked out."

"How old were the kids in your care?"

"Two and four when I started with them."

He glanced down at the paper in front of him, which she could see was a copy of her résumé. "And you were with them for two and half years? Why'd you leave?"

"My parents were in an accident and killed." She could almost say it now without having her throat close up. "My sister needed me. She was in her senior year of high school. I took a semester off to settle my parents' affairs, and to be there for her until she graduated."

"It must have been tough." A gruffness in his voice reminded her he'd lost his wife just over a year ago.

"We had each other, which helped." But it had still been the toughest year of her life.

"Right." He cleared his throat. "So you haven't had care of a baby?"

"Not as young as thirteen months, no, but I'm sure I can manage. I have a master's in Child Development, and I love kids. In fact, my sister is expecting, so in six weeks I'll be an aunt for the first time."

He showed no change of expression at the mention of a pending birth. From mild to effusive, most people showed some form of acknowledgment. It made her wonder about the relationship between him and his son, and why Trace was only now taking custody of the boy.

She knew from the agency that he was a widower, that the baby had survived the accident that had killed his mother, and that Trace's mother-in-law had had care of the baby until a week ago.

"So what's the deal with you? Why are you just now getting custody of your son?" She put the question out there.

A dark eyebrow lifted at her bluntness.

She smiled and lifted one shoulder in a half-shrug. "I believe in open communication. Life is simpler that way." She kept her smile in place and waited. So sue her. She wanted to know, and she'd found asking usually netted answers.

After a moment he answered. "I've always had custody. My in-laws were just helping out until I got settled in a new location."

It took thirteen months? But she didn't voice the thought. Obviously there was something more involved than a simple move. And there would be, of course. A cop and a newborn were hardly a good fit on their own. Plus, something in his voice told her he hadn't been completely comfortable with the arrangement. She took an educated guess.

"I imagine it was a comfort to your in-laws to have their grandson close while they dealt with losing their daughter."

He leaned back in his seat, his brawny forearms

crossed over the wide expanse of his chest. He eyed her suspiciously. "Most people assume I was taking advantage of my in-laws. Not that it's any of their business."

From his defensive posture Nikki guessed "most people" weren't entirely wrong. But she also heard a note of hurt pride. Five years as a teacher had taught her to read people, be they little or big or somewhere in between. For a man of his control, who made duty a way of life, a shadow on his honor would bite big-time.

"Of course." She acknowledged his distancing comment, and then completely disregarded it. "Death is never easy on a family," she sympathized. "But from my experience once a grandmother has a baby in her care it takes a bomb and a crowbar to pry the child loose."

Sheriff Oliver choked on an indrawn breath.

"Oops." Nikki bit her lower lip. Her sister continually warned Nikki that some people didn't appreciate her chronic bluntness. "Not sensitive enough?"

Trace threw back his head and laughed out loud. Something he did all too rarely. He ran a hand over his face as he fought to regain his cool.

"You're very insightful," was all he said. Actually, the truth laid somewhere in the middle of what people thought and the need for a crowbar.

But, Lord, he did appreciate a little blunt honesty. The empathy was harder to accept. From the huskiness in her voice earlier, he had no doubt she still mourned her parents.

"Don't be so hard on yourself," she urged him in

earnest. "It couldn't have been easy handling a newborn on a sheriff's schedule."

"I wasn't a sheriff then. I transferred nine months ago. Before that I was a homicide detective, attached to a multinational task force."

"Sounds important."

"It was. And, as you said, difficult to juggle with a newborn. My mother-in-law offered to help out by taking Carmichael. I was grateful for her aid. But just over a week ago she had a stroke, and my father-in-law moved them back to Michigan, where her family could help with her care and support. It's just me and my son now."

Trace shifted in his chair. He didn't know why he felt the need to explain things to her he hadn't shared with anyone else.

Maybe talking was easier because of the understanding he saw in her intelligent amber eyes, or maybe her honesty called to something in him. Whatever it was, it needed to stop now.

"Carmichael?" she echoed. "I thought his name was Michael?"

"No, it's Carmichael. A family name on my mother-in-law's side."

"Oh. The agency has Michael on my paperwork."

"Then they have it wrong. He's been called Carmichael since he was born." Trace hated the name, but he'd agreed to it to make his wife happy. They probably would have shortened the name if she'd lived. But she'd died. "His mother chose the name."

"Right. Continuity is a fine family tradition." She

carefully kept her tone even. He literally saw the struggle it cost her.

"But you don't like it?" He shouldn't test her when she'd made such an effort at politeness, but he couldn't resist.

She struggled for another moment, her smile both brave and patently false. Finally tact gave way to that refreshing honesty.

"It's just so much *name* for a baby," she said in a rush. "They have to learn to walk before they can run, and that's not just physically. Their little psyches need to grow and develop just like their bodies."

So much passion for his son, and she hadn't even met him. Just what any father would want in a nanny.

Right.

"Just be careful not to let guilt motivate your decisions."

The words hit him like a fist to the gut. This was what he got for sharing. "What are you talking about?"

"It's called survivor's guilt. And it causes rational people to make irrational choices. It's just something to be aware of. You think you're honoring her because she can't be here to raise Carmichael. But what she'd really want is for you to love him and raise him the best you can."

"Love the child, honor the mother?"

"Yes. It's that simple."

"Your life may be that easy, Ms. Rhodes, but you know nothing of mine. Don't presume you know my motive for anything." Hearing the harshness of his tone, he took a breath. But on this he needed to be clear. "Carmichael is the focus here. Never attempt to psychoanalyze me."

"Of course." She bit her lip. "I'm sorry. I only meant to help."

"Yeah, well, if there's one thing I've learned since becoming a father it's that nothing is simple anymore. Life has become one complication after another."

She nodded. "Families are complicated. Love is what makes it work."

Good Lord. If that were true, he was in a world of trouble. Rather than dwell on his emotional shortcomings, he switched back to her comments on Child Development.

"I thought you didn't work with infants."

"I don't. But in kindergarten they're still growing and learning when they get to me."

She shifted in her seat, smoothing a hand down a cotton-clad thigh, and then completely changed the subject on him. "I understand you've already had two nannies come and go in the past week. What was the problem with them?"

He frowned. "Why do you want to know?"

"It'll help me to know what you're looking for."

"Right. I guess that makes sense. The first couldn't handle the schedule. She was too concerned with disruptions to her time off and the distance from San Diego. The second seemed set in her ways. She had tried-and-true doctrines and regimens, and she made it clear it would be her way or no way. I chose no way."

"Good for you." Approval beamed at him from across the room, making him feel twelve feet tall. She was a pretty woman, with even features, a plump mouth and a peaches-and-cream complexion, but what really made her attractive was her animation. This woman lived life; it showed in her perpetual smile and those amazing amber eyes.

She lit the room with energy, just sitting on his slate-blue sofa. He watched as she tossed a flow of honey-brown hair over her shoulder. A slight frown created a furrow between slim dark brows.

"Sadly, a lot of parents want just such an arrangement. It's almost as if they prefer to be visitors in their children's lives rather than participants." Her tone made it clear what she thought of those misguided parents.

Must be nice to live in her merry little world. He knew the truth. "I'm in law enforcement, Ms. Rhodes. I can tell you parents often cause less damage to a kid just by virtue of their absence."

"You're right, of course. But that's not what I meant."

"I know what you meant. I've been a visitor in my son's life for more than a year. But that's over. I'm responsible for him now. I'll decide what's best for him."

And chatting up a kindergartener teacher, no matter how blunt and vivacious, wasn't going to get the job done.

Was she the nanny for him?

On the surface she was too young, too overqualified, too inexperienced. It didn't take a master's degree to change a diaper, but it took someone who'd been around babies to know the difference between a fever due to teething or an illness. Something he'd learned just this week.

On the other hand it was a job, and the budget cuts did have a lot of teachers looking for employment.

"Ms. Rhodes—"

"Please," she interjected, "call me Nikki."

"Ms. Rhodes." It was better that way. Better to keep everything professional. "When can you start?"

CHAPTER TWO

"WHEN can you start?"

As soon as Trace said the words the cell phone on the coffee table rang and a cry echoed from down the hall. He stopped and reached for the phone.

"I'm sorry," he said. "I have to get this. Do you mind checking on the baby for me?"

"Right." Nikki surged to her feet and tugged on the short hem of her vest. She had the job! So she wasn't keen to be working for a control fiend—she'd get to stay close to Amanda, and that was what mattered. Nikki could hardly wait to tell her sister. "Which room?"

He nodded toward the hall. "Last door on the right."

Turned out Nikki needed the directions, because the crying had stopped. She found that odd. In her experience babies wanting attention usually got louder, not quieter.

She pushed open the half-closed door and peered inside. The room held only a crib and a dressing table/dresser set made of fine oak. The walls were white, the sheets and blankets a dark navy. There were no toys in sight.

A brown-haired, solemn-eyed baby sat quietly in the crib.

Nikki's heart wrenched. She'd never seen such a sad child in her life. Poor baby. He must really be missing his grandmother.

"Hello, Carmichael," she greeted him softly as she approached the crib. "I'm Nikki."

She rested her forearms on the wooden railing and smiled, prepared to chat for a moment before plucking him from his bed.

He watched her with those big sad eyes—green, like his father's—but made no move toward or away from her.

"Carmichael is a lot of name to live up to. Someday I'm sure you'll rate every syllable." Letting him get used to her, she reached out and wiggled his little nose. "In the meantime, you look more like a Mickey to me."

The corners of his mouth turned up in a tiny smile.

Pleased by his reaction, she asked, "You like that? You like the name Mickey? I like it, too." She gave his nose another wiggle. "Are you a fan of the mouse? He'd certainly bring a little color to the room, wouldn't he?"

The boy rolled over and crawled to the side of the crib, using the rails to climb up. Once he stood opposite her, he turned shy again, eying her warily. She kept her smile in place, showing him he had nothing to fear.

Her patience was rewarded when he suddenly poked her in the nose.

"Uh-oh," she said in mock alarm. "You got my nose."

He grinned and poked her again.

"Oh, look at you—you got me again. I'm going to get you back." She wiggled his nose one more time.

And he giggled.

The happy sound sent a buzz of triumph through Nikki. She'd made him laugh! The poor baby needed joy in his life, especially with a father ready to control his every move. Nikki readily admitted over-controlling parents were a hot button for her. If the location and the live-in facilities didn't make this the perfect job she'd be tempted to turn it down. She didn't look forward to working for a man with no *give* in his life.

Mickey raised his arms for her to pick him up, and her heart twisted in her chest. Here was another reason for her to stay. One smile made it worth her while.

She lifted him into a huge hug. One arm went around her neck and he laid his head on her shoulder. A lump grew in her throat. There was no feeling in the world like the soft weight of a baby cuddled trustingly in your arms.

She turned and found Trace framed in the open doorway.

Nikki met his green gaze over the baby's head. From the raw emotion in the jade depths she knew he'd heard Mickey's laughter.

"He likes you." Trace came no further than the threshold, his gaze locked on his son in her arms. "Good. That was Dispatch. There's been an accident. I have to go in. Can you start now? I tried Russ again, and he's still not answering, so I need a sitter."

When he raised his glance to her, his expression was closed again. For just a moment his guard had slipped. Now it was back in full force.

"Sure I can watch him. How long will you be?"

Mickey sat up in her arms and looked at his father, almost as if the baby understood what they were talking about. He couldn't, of course, but tone and undercurrents were strong in the air. He probably felt the tension pulsing through the room. She bounced him in her arms.

"I don't know. It could be late." Trace's shuttered expression didn't change.

"Okay, I'll call my sister and let her know I'll be late."

Trace gave one sharp nod. "Okay. I've got to change, then I'll show you where everything is."

"I'll change Mick—Carmichael's diaper and meet you in the living room."

Trace nodded and disappeared down the hall.

Nikki laid Mickey down on the changing table. He made no move to twist or turn away. He simply lay still and watched her. His listlessness tore at her soul.

She chatted to him as she cleaned him up. He took in every word she said, but showed no reaction.

She suspected his grandmother, in her love and loss, had wrapped him in Bubble Wrap, cared for him to the extent she'd smothered the life from him. And Nikki feared his father, obviously a man of discipline and control, would go too far in the opposite direction, until all sense of laughter and spontaneity were lost to this sad little boy.

As soon as Mickey had laughed she'd known she'd have to find a way to work with the father, because this baby needed her. Mickey needed joy and discovery, activity and a sense of adventure. She'd learned to embrace life, and she wanted to share the world with him.

"You went for an interview and you're starting now?" Her sister's droll response to Nikki's explanation of where she'd be for the evening restated the paradox of Nikki's unorthodox hiring process. "Sounds like a pretty desperate situation."

"It is. But it's in Paradise Pines, so I'll be close to you, and it's live-in so I can move out of your place. It's the perfect set-up for our needs right now." Nikki settled deeper into the corner of the couch, the phone tucked between her shoulder and her ear, Mickey in her lap. "And you should see this little boy. Mickey is so sweet, but so sad. I'm sure he misses his grandparents, but his despondency seems to be habitual more than incidental. He lost his mother; his grandparents lost their daughter. I don't think he's ever known happiness."

"Oh, Nikki, this does not sound good. You know you don't have to move out."

"You're being sweet, but we both know I do need to move out. You and Dan need this time together. Besides, I'm a teacher. Morally and professionally it's my job to do something when I see a child in need."

There was a short telling silence. Then a sigh sounded down the line. "Nikki, do you really know what you're getting into?"

"Not at all." And yet Mickey's sadness had awakened all her protective instincts.

"Amanda, he's thirteen months old and can't walk." She ran her fingers through his silky brown hair, the curls so soft and fine they felt like down feathers. Mickey looked up at her with his solemn eyes. Her heart wrenched. "He doesn't even put his feet out when I set him down. His grandmother must have carried him all the time."

"Isn't all this his father's problem?"

"That's just it. Trace is new at all of this. I'm not sure he'll recognize the problems. In fact, he may make things worse. He's all about control and structure, and Mickey is well behaved so there's nothing for Trace to question."

"But, Nikki," Amanda calmly rationalized, "what can you do?"

"Trace Oliver is a good sheriff, which means he's dutiful and honorable. I'm sure he wants to do what's best for Mickey. He's just clueless what that is. I can teach him."

"Ha!" The rude exclamation tickled Nikki's ear. "I'm due in a month and a half, remember? I've read every book on the subject over the past seven months and I can tell you with little exaggeration that there are twelve thousand 'right ways.' Everyone has an opinion, and some of them are really out there."

"Yeah." Nikki smiled. Her sister did like to know what to expect. She took after Mom in that way. "But this is what I'm trained in. I know I can help Trace and Mickey."

"I have no doubt you can. I've never seen anyone better with kids than you. Because you care, and they can sense it. But that's the problem." Amanda's concern reached through the connection. "You give too much of yourself. This whole thing sounds like a heart-trap to me."

"So you don't think I should do it?"

Another sigh. "I know it will haunt you if you don't, but I'm worried about you getting hurt."

Yeah, that worried Nikki, too. But she'd promised herself on her eighteenth birthday she wouldn't live life afraid to feel. She gave herself to life, heart and soul. Sometimes that meant she got hurt, but it also meant her life was full of rich emotions and lasting memories.

"Life isn't meant to be pain-free."

"Nikki," Amanda said gently, "are you sure this isn't the backlash of your relationship with Mom?"

The question sent sharp pangs of sorrow and regret through Nikki. The frayed state of her relationship with her mother at the time of her death would forever eat at Nikki's soul. She hated, *hated* that her last conversation with Mom had been an argument.

"I can't say it doesn't strike a chord. At a time when he should be reaching for independence, Mickey is totally despondent. If he doesn't develop some spirit he'll never stand a chance."

"You mean, against his father?"

"No. Don't put words in my mouth." Was that how she really felt? Nikki shook her head. She didn't know. She hadn't spent enough time with either of them to make that call. "This is what I know—if I can bring them together now, then they'll have a foundation to build on that will hold them together when the times get rough."

After stating her concern one more time, Amanda ended the call. Nikki understood her sister's hesitation.

She'd defended him to Amanda, but Trace had barely looked at Mickey, much less touched him before leaving, which burned Nikki's hide. Somehow she needed to find a way to bring father and son alive, to teach them to love one another.

Two months. She'd give herself the summer to make a difference, then she'd re-evaluate her situation.

Mickey shyly petted her hair. She sighed and shifted him in her arms. She had a bad feeling she'd lose a part of her heart this summer.

Long after he'd expected to be home that night, Trace pulled into his driveway. The sight of a light inside sent an odd sense of warmth through him. He'd missed that sign of homecoming.

The thought of Ms. Rhodes waiting inside sent an altogether different type of heat surging through his blood. But he quickly blanked off the unruly attraction and pushed his way out of the SUV.

Ms. Rhodes was so far off-limits she might as well be on Mars.

The balmy night air flowed over him as the pine-scented breeze lifted the hair off his brow. Unlocking the front door, he stepped inside and traded fragrant pine for the savory aroma of roast chicken. His stomach growled, reminding him of the hours since his last meal.

He moved to the counter separating the kitchen from the living room to place his keys in their regulated dish, and found a note saying a plate was made up for him in the microwave.

She'd cooked for him.

He checked it out. Chicken, rice and a melody of mixed vegetables. It looked damn good. Again that mysterious warmth glowed in his depths. He cursed.

Hell, man, get a grip. What? Was he going soft at the ripe old age of thirty-five? How could a home-cooked meal and a baby in the house throw him so off-stride? So he had a son to raise. He'd do it like he did everything else—with discipline and structure.

Which in no way explained why he'd hired Ms. Rhodes.

With her short pants, flimsy sandals and figure-hugging navy vest, she'd looked more prepared for a day at the races than a job interview. And her cavalier "it worked out" attitude, along with her schedule with the Hendersons, spoke of a spontaneity he found untenable.

But she'd made Carmichael laugh.

Forking up a bite of chicken, Trace stood over the back of the couch and looked at Carmichael, asleep in Nikki Rhodes's arms. The four-car pile-up on the inter-state freeway had taken hours to clear up and document. The Highway Patrol would do the forensics on the fatalities, but his men had been first on scene, so he'd been responsible for traffic control and dealing with the injured.

Death. There was no escaping it.

But then he was used to loss in one form or another. His wife to a car accident, much like the one tonight. His mother had just left—abandoning him and his dad when Trace was ten. And his dad had died two years before Trace married Donna.

Yeah, good old Mom and Dad. Never a demonstrative man, his father had taught Trace all about integrity and honor, but he'd frowned on any display of emotion. Which was why Trace's mom had left his dad. Left them. She'd used to say he was just like his dad.

He didn't know how to love.

Hell, he'd had no business marrying Donna. But she'd pushed for it and he'd found her companionable enough. Plus they'd been great in bed. He'd thought that was the best he was going to get.

Of course she'd wanted more from him than he could give. They'd fought. Often. Then Donna had landed on the idea of a baby. With his dad as an example of what kind of father Trace would make, he'd been against it. Especially when they were so often at odds with each other. She'd gotten pregnant anyway.

After his initial anger, he'd settled down. She'd been so excited, and he'd figured with a baby to focus her attention on she'd get off his case. God, she'd deserved better.

No, he should never have married. He wouldn't make the mistake again.

He pretended the thought had nothing to do with why his gaze sought out Nikki Rhodes. Seeing her and

Carmichael cuddled together, Trace envied the peace on his son's face.

God, her porcelain skin looked as soft as the baby's. Trace fought the urge to touch, to test for himself. That was a no-go. As his employee she'd be strictly off-limits.

It shouldn't be a problem. He ruled his body; his hormones didn't. He rarely did anything without careful thought and planning.

The bottom line was he needed Ms. Rhodes.

She'd made Carmichael smile—giggle, even. For that alone she was worth any discomfort he felt. What kind of father would he be if he put his personal well-being above the very real needs of his son?

There'd have to be ground rules.

She was too much of a free spirit, and, where he appreciated the blunt honesty she'd displayed, her unpredictability would drive him nuts. His uncharacteristic openness with her spoke of how easily she'd twisted him up.

Love was not an automatic response. He didn't get all gooey-eyed or mushy inside when he looked at his son. He did feel a sense of duty. He'd made the decision to have a child and he'd do his best by him. Even if his best didn't include love. He'd survived without it. So would his son.

CHAPTER THREE

"YOU'RE home." The sleep husky voice came from the depths of the couch.

He looked down into honey-brown eyes, felt the warmth rising and turned away.

"Yeah, thanks for staying." Glancing at his empty plate, he saw he'd eaten every bite. He set the plate on the island countertop. "Let me take Carmichael to bed."

"Poor little guy missed you tonight." Nikki shifted around until she half sat, with Carmichael draped over her lap. "He wouldn't go to sleep in his crib. I think having a stranger here at bedtime threw him off."

"It wasn't you," Trace assured her grimly as he lifted his tiny son into his arms, careful not to wake him. "He hasn't slept well since he came here. Hang on, I'll be back in a minute."

He carried his light burden to the nursery and laid the boy down gently. He placed a toy giraffe next to the baby and tucked them both in with a soft navy blanket. Carmichael stirred. Trace stood over him until he settled, then returned to the living room.

Trace thanked God he had the garage converted out back. At least he and Ms. Rhodes wouldn't have to share the house. He'd purposely looked for a property with a detached extra room or granny flat. The division of space served a couple of purposes. One, it preserved his reputation and that of any lady he hired, and two, it defined the barrier between employer and employee and established boundaries for personal space.

Nikki was in the kitchen, cleaning his dinner dishes. Quite the domestic picture.

"Leave them," he told her. "I'll get to them later."

She looked over her shoulder at him and smiled. "They're already done." She opened the cupboard to the left of the sink and placed the plate inside, then turned to face him as she dried her hands with a dishcloth. "It was no trouble."

"We have to talk."

She nodded, folded the cloth over the edge of the sink and followed him to the living room. "It's pretty late. It must have been bad tonight."

"Bad enough." He grimly dismissed the accident that had claimed two lives. A lawman couldn't afford to make it personal. "That's not what we need to talk about."

"Of course." She leaned forward. "Carmichael is such a sweet little boy, but so sad. He must miss his grandparents a lot."

"He asks after them, yes. They've been the constant in his life. He has to get past that."

"And he will, as you replace them in his affections."

He frowned, unnerved at being anyone's emotional stable. But this was his son, so he put steel in his backbone and strengthened his resolve.

"Bonding will take a bit of time," she continued, right through his moment of panic. "Especially with a schedule as erratic as yours."

That stung. "I'm doing the best I can."

"Are you?" She flushed and held up a placating hand. "I'm sorry. I understand yours isn't a nine-to-five job, but it'll really help if you can find some time during the day to spend together. That's usually easiest during a meal, or at bath or bedtime."

"I know the importance of an established schedule." How exactly had he become the one on the defense?

"I'm sure you do. And it's early days for the two of you together. I'm sure we'll find a system that works for all of us."

He appreciated her enthusiasm even as he resisted it. "Sit down, Ms. Rhodes. We have a few ground rules to discuss."

"Of course." The words were terse, reminding him that, as a teacher, she was more used to making rules than following them.

"First of all, there should be no touching."

Her brow furrowed and a question came into her eyes.

"You're an attractive woman," he clarified. "And I'm a healthy adult male. I've noticed you're demonstrative. You talk with your hands and you express emotion by touching. We need to maintain a professional relationship, so no touching."

She inclined her head in acknowledgment. "That makes sense. What else?"

"I don't need or want you to cook for me. No getting cozy around the kitchen table or snoozing on the couch."

"Cozy?" She actually sounded offended by the notion. Perching on the arm of the couch, she crossed her arms over her chest. "I have to cook for the baby and me anyway. It's just as easy to include enough for you. In fact, it's harder to cook for one and a half than for three, so it's just plain wasteful not to include you. If you don't want me to leave it warming in the oven, fine. I'll tuck the food into the refrigerator and you can dig it out. As for snoozing on the couch—you were late. I fell asleep."

Frowning, she reached for the baby blanket she'd used as a throw and began to fold it. When she continued much of the defiance was missing. "From the sound of your schedule that's likely to happen again, so how do you suggest we handle the problem?"

Good question.

"I'll put a travel crib in your rooms out back. If you get sleepy, you can take Carmichael with you and I'll pick him up when I get home."

"That's disruptive for the baby."

"Yeah." His gaze roamed from her Blushed Rose toenails to her two-inch gold hoop earrings. "Well, I think it's best. I'd also like you to wear a uniform. It doesn't have to be formal, just keep to black and white."

Nikki shifted the blanket she'd folded from her lap

to her chest and crossed her arms. "Maybe you should write down all these rules so I don't forget them."

He lifted a brow at her tone. "I'll let that slide, because it's late and we're both tired. But know this: I don't believe in ignoring problems. I believe in addressing the issue to prevent further problems from arising."

"Now, see, I have a different philosophy. Some problems, yes, need to be resolved right away. Others, if you ignore them, often go away."

"Or someone else handles them for you."

"Sometimes, and it's lovely when that happens. Other times new info comes to light which changes the situation so the original problem goes away." She stood and gathered her belongings on the way to the door, where she stopped and met his gaze straight-on. "I don't think you need to worry about us getting cozy around the dinner table." She hooked her purse over her shoulder. "See you tomorrow."

Nikki purposely timed her arrival for 7:00 a.m. the next morning. Not a minute before or a minute after. She'd learned her lesson about punctuality when it came to Sheriff Oliver.

As good as he looked in his skin, she was sure encountering him half-naked again would bend more than one of his rules.

She needn't have worried. He met her at the door fully dressed. He took her suitcase and set it inside the door.

"Carmichael is still sleeping," he told her. "And I

got a call from Dispatch so I have to go." He grabbed his keys from the bowl on the counter and headed back to the door.

Oh, my, he did look fine in his uniform.

He wore it with an easy air of command that made the olive-green pants and khaki short-sleeved shirt—accessorized with holster and gun—downright sexy. The confidence and authority he projected made her nerves tingle.

She told herself it was in annoyance for his desertion even as she caught herself staring.

He met her gaze. "I'll show you your rooms tonight."

"Wait." She stepped into his path. "What about the time you're going to spend with Carmichael?"

"It'll have to be tonight." He walked around her. "I'll try to check in during the day. I left my numbers by the phone if there's an emergency."

The door closed behind him and Nikki found herself alone in the quiet house. That *so* had not gone how she'd expected.

That night, Nikki followed Trace Oliver's broad-shouldered, slim-hipped saunter to the garage behind his house. She eyed his chiseled profile, waiting for the right moment to address her concerns. She'd had all day to plot her course of action. She'd try to catch him in a good mood, but if that failed she'd have to risk the fallout. Mickey had needs and she meant to see them met.

"These will be your rooms." Trace opened the door and gestured her inside.

Head held high, she squeezed past him, inhaling soap, mint and man, an intoxicating combination. It was enough to distract her from her surroundings—until the wheels of her suitcase bumped up against the threshold and stopped. With a small tug, she proceeded into the room.

He'd been polite but distant since arriving home. Mickey was sleeping, so Trace was taking the opportunity to show her where she'd be staying.

The garage had been converted into a studio apartment. A large living area included a small kitchen in the far right corner. A full bath occupied the far left corner, with a closet dividing the two. Like the main house, the furnishings here were modern, simplistic, in dark gray and burgundy.

Yeah, a few feminine touches might bring it up to the level of an impersonal hotel room. Not a problem. She needed to clear out of her sister's place anyway. The infusion of her things would brighten this space, bring a warmth and hominess to the small suite.

She moved deeper into the room and caught her reflection in the full-length mirror on the closet door. Intent on fostering the professional relationship they'd agreed upon—and he'd outlined it in excruciating detail—she'd dressed in a pencil-slim skirt that ended two inches above her knees and a fitted vest both in black. For herself, she'd paired the severe clothing with a romantic white cotton shirt, ruffled at the scooped neck and capped sleeves. Black sandals completed the outfit.

Catching sight of his reflection behind her, she felt

a punch to the gut. He looked as good now as he had this morning—better, actually. Being a little rumpled made him appear more approachable.

Not wanting to be caught staring, she quickly diverted her attention back to the room.

"This is really very nice. Is there wood for the fireplace?" Oh, great save. Like she needed a fire in late June.

"By the shed outside, to the left. But you probably won't be here long enough to use it."

"What do you mean?" Miffed, Nikki tried and failed to keep the bite out of the question. "I'm playing by the rules." She gestured to her uniform of black and white.

His intense gaze rolled over her until his eyes met hers. "Right. But we both know this is a temporary arrangement at best."

"Why do you say that?" she demanded. "I assure you I truly care about Mickey, and I'm committed to staying until—"

Whoa. She cut herself off as her mind caught up with her mouth. She couldn't tell him she intended staying until father and son bonded. Already she knew he'd take her interference as well as a cat took to water: with a whole lot of resistance and no discernible gratitude for the effort involved. He only accepted her presence now because Mickey liked her. That was where she needed to channel her efforts.

"Until what, Ms. Rhodes? He starts school? Can stay home alone? Begins to drive? You won't be here through the end of the year, let alone any of those milestones."

And there was a fine sample of opposition. Leaving her suitcase against the wall, she plopped into a soft gray armchair, planted her elbows on the arms, and got to the heart of the matter.

"Why did you hire me if you're ready to push me out the door?"

He surprised her when he gave up his position of power to sit across from her. "First of all, because you're a teacher, not a nanny. You're going to go back to teaching the first chance you get. It's obvious when you talk about it that you love your job. Second, I can see you do care about Carmichael. More important, he likes you. But let's not kid ourselves. You're a meddler, Ms. Rhodes. You can't help yourself. And I can't tolerate being manipulated. I have a high-pressure, high-exposure job. I need to know my child is being cared for to my specifications, and to find peace when I walk through my door at the end of my shift."

Okay, she gave him points for insightfulness and, yeah, she understood the whole peace-in-his-own-home thing. Her mother had always wanted peace. Nikki considered it overrated. Give her loud and loving every time. Laughter wasn't a quiet commodity.

As for meddling—he was right. She couldn't deny it. But the man had serious emotional issues. She intended to help him and Mickey find a connection. If he preferred for her to be up-front about it, she could do up-front.

"I prefer to think of it as caring about people." Earnest in her concern, she leaned forward. "I care about Carmichael. You didn't even stop to check on him this evening. So, yeah, I'm going to meddle. He needs you, so what's it going to take to get you to stand steady for him?"

Trace's dark brows slammed together. "You're out of line."

"Blame yourself." Nikki waved his irritation aside. "You hired me to take care of Carmichael. To me that means more than changing diapers and heating bottles. His emotional welfare is as important as his physical welfare. Why are you so afraid of emotion?"

He surprised her with an immediate response.

"I'm not afraid of emotion, Ms. Rhodes, I'm just not very good at it."

Nikki blinked at the unexpected reply. How sad if that was true. The total lack of feeling in his expression revealed he believed it.

"And it's easier to back away than try?" she guessed.

"I've tried." A shadow of pain came and went in his level gaze. The flash of vulnerability convinced her of his claim more than the stoic words. "That's how I know I'm no good at it."

She could tell it had cost him. Still, she had to press. For him and for Mickey. "Well, it's time to try again. Can I be frank with you? Mickey's development is stunted. You know I have a master's in Child Development. He's behind in speech, in walking, in his motor skills."

His eyes narrowed to slits. "You're saying my child is slow?"

"No. He's smart, and actually quick to catch on to new things. But he just sits, and he always wants to be held."

"His grandmother was very protective of him," he said slowly, his mind obviously at work. "Whenever I visited she held him all the time. I thought it was because she was afraid I would take him away. She must have coddled him to the extent he did little for himself."

"It's sad, isn't it?" she asked, compassion illuminating her features. "She'd lost her daughter. Her grandson was all she had left of her child. She hung on to him with all her might, and ended up impeding his progress instead of nurturing his growth."

"She held on so tight she may have irreparably damaged his ongoing development. That's not sad, that's negligent. And I let it happen."

"It's not necessary to place blame," Nikki assured him. "What matters is what you do now. Your son needs you. We talked about you setting time aside each day to spend with him. When would be best for you?"

"I've already explained my days are chaotic in the extreme. I keep a schedule, but I'm always on call. I can't give you a set time."

"Come on." She sighed, her understanding slipping. "That's a cop-out."

"Be careful, Ms. Rhodes." Dark color stained his cheeks and he fixed a fierce frown on her.

"Good parents make time for their kids."

"I'm aware of that, but—"

"No *buts*. Everyone's busy. We'll just work at it until

we find a time. We'll start with breakfast. How does bacon and eggs sound?"

He shook his head. "I usually grab something at the station."

Now he was just being difficult.

"Good. You'll be able to focus all your attention on Mickey. You can have a cup of coffee while you feed him."

"I'm the employer, Ms. Rhodes. I make the rules."

"Yeah, I've noticed you're big on rules. It's all about structure and control for you, isn't it? So you'll understand the benefit of a regular schedule for your son."

He scowled, but she saw he was thinking about her comments. Good. She rose and went to the door.

"Thanks for showing me my rooms. I'd like to get settled in, but I'll see you at breakfast. Seven o'clock. I'll cook."

He blew her off again the next morning. When she came in, he was strapping on his utility belt, getting ready to walk out the door.

He nodded to the baby monitor. "Carmichael is still sleeping. He should be up soon. He slept through the night for the first time since getting here. I have to go."

She propped her hands on her hips. "What about our date?"

His laser green gaze sliced to her, and she cringed inwardly at her unfortunate word-choice. The word probably added to his irritation at being questioned at all.

"Our *appointment* will have to wait until tomorrow.

The Mayor called for a breakfast meeting. Was I supposed to tell him I couldn't make it because I had to feed my son?"

"You say that as if feeding your son isn't important." Walking to the table for the baby monitor, she sent him an aggravated glare. "Did you even suggest an alternative time?"

"No." He shrugged. "We often meet over breakfast. We're busy men, it's easiest to get our session out of the way early."

"And that was fine when you were on your own. Now you have a son who needs your attention."

"He'll get it tomorrow morning." He grabbed his keys and headed for the door. He slid on mirrored shades, which added an extra layer of stern to his tough visage. "Don't attempt to interfere with my work, Ms. Rhodes. You won't like the results."

Nikki fumed as he closed the door on her—figuratively and literally.

She stormed into the kitchen and took her ire out on innocent pots and pans.

"Oh, shoot. Wait!" She went running for the door, to catch Trace before he left, but when she stepped out on the deck it was to watch his SUV disappear down the street.

"Dang." Stubborn man. He'd riled her both last night and this morning, so she'd forgotten to ask about the car seat for Carmichael. She assumed it must be in Trace's vehicle, because she hadn't found it when she went through the house and garage yesterday. There was no stroller, either. Nor playpen or walker. The only baby items were the crib and dressing table and a highchair.

He needed to pick up the necessities from his in-laws' place or buy new ones, because she and Mickey were prisoners without them. Back in the kitchen, she frowned at the cupboards, reminded they were also low on groceries. She began to plot her evening. There was more than one twenty-four-hour superstore in the county.

If she had to call 911 to get his attention, she and Trace would be visiting one before the night ended.

CHAPTER FOUR

NIKKI was ready for Trace when he got home at seven that evening. She sat alone at the dining-room table, her purse in front of her, along with a small cooler of food. The elusive Russ was playing with Mickey in his room down the hall.

She'd covered dinner and a sitter; she didn't want Trace to have any wiggle room to get out of going shopping. Mickey was as sweet as could be, and a good baby, but he expected to be held all the time. Nikki literally couldn't get anything done. And without a car seat or stroller, she remained housebound.

It might be unfair to expect Trace to shop after a twelve-hour day, but expecting her to care for a baby without the proper equipment was equally unreasonable.

He walked in the door and over to the dish to drop in his keys. He glanced around, then looked at her.

"What's up? Are you going someplace? Hey, I'm sorry I'm late." He rubbed a hand over the back of his neck in a weary gesture. "Time just disappears. Is Carmichael sleeping?"

"No. I hired Russ to watch him tonight. Carmichael needs some things. You and I are going shopping."

"Not tonight." Dark brows lowered in a frown. "I'm tired and I'm hungry. We'll go tomorrow."

"We're going tonight," she insisted. "I've only been here two days, and I already know not to trust the promise of tomorrow."

His scowl darkened, but he couldn't deny the allegation. "I thought I made it clear how I feel about being manipulated."

"Then don't force it on me." She patted the cooler and recited the list of items Carmichael required. "I've packed you dinner. Believe me, I wouldn't ask you to go out if I didn't really need these things to care for him properly. I'm tired, too, but we need to go tonight. How did you even get Carmichael home without a car seat?"

He looked pained. "There was one. It was too small, so I took it down to the station to have on hand in case of an emergency." He sighed. "Do I have time for a shower and change of clothes?"

Relieved to have his co-operation, she grinned. "If you hurry."

"Do you want a modular unit for a playpen, or will the portable crib work?" Trace asked as they stood in the baby aisle of the superstore.

"Oh, do they have modular units here?" Nikki

stepped back to view the merchandise better. "Where? Does it list the dimensions?"

"I don't see them here. A friend has one. I can find out where he got it, or order it online, but you'd have to wait."

She took in their two carts, swollen with large boxes. It contained a fortune. "Oh, yeah, we don't have to get everything tonight. I wasn't thinking of the expense."

"Let me worry about the expense." Injured pride added bite to his response. "I'd rather finish it tonight. I can afford whatever is needed for my son."

"Of course. I didn't mean to imply you couldn't." Maybe she could use that pride to motivate him on an emotional level. "Thank you for coming out tonight. I've really been stuck these past couple of days. Carmichael is a good baby but—"

"He wants to be held," Trace finished, and she met his gaze in a moment of shared understanding. "I know."

"Let's go to the toys. He needs to become engaged in activities that hold his attention. Russ brought over some of his niece's blocks. He says Carmichael will play with them for an hour or more."

"Huh?" Trace made a show of turning toward the toys. "Let's get us some blocks."

She laughed, and quickly caught up to him. "When are you going to pick up the rest of his stuff?"

He looked blank. "What do you mean?"

"His stuff. For his room. Toys, stuffed animals, wall hangings. Things with color and form to inspire his mind—that stuff."

"Oh. There wasn't any of that in what my father-in-law brought."

"So M— Carmichael has no stuff? That's kind of sad." Shocked and saddened by the revelation, Nikki spoke without thinking, but regretted her lack of forethought when she saw the humor fade from his face. She tried to save the moment. "But, hey, that means you get to choose his stuff."

"Me?" A shadow passed over his features. "I wouldn't know where to start."

"It's easy," she encouraged him. "What did you have in your room as a kid?"

"Here are the blocks." Pushing into the toy aisle, he made a point of studying the displays. Finally he said, "My room looked pretty much like Carmichael's, except with a bed instead of a crib."

"Oh, Trace," she whispered. "You're breaking my heart."

He glanced at her and his eyes softened. "No need," he assured her. "You don't miss what you never knew."

Caught by his compelling jade gaze, she moved closer. "You have a chance to give him something you never had."

He nodded, and then moved his gaze down to his side. "You're touching me, Ms. Rhodes."

So she was. Both arms were wrapped around his strong arm. Muscles flexed under her fingers as he carefully stepped away.

"Sorry," she said.

"Yeah." Reaching for a box of blocks, he changed the

subject. Relieved, she followed his lead. For such a tough character he showed vulnerability at the oddest moments. It was clear to her that he needed Mickey as much as Mickey needed him.

She blinked away weak tears. She'd have to stay strong if she meant to help them find each other.

Back at the house, she checked on Mickey while Trace and Russ unloaded everything from the SUV. After Russ took off, she asked Trace, "How did the other nannies make do without this gear?"

He shrugged. "They weren't around long."

"It was the rules, right? You probably scared them away with all your rules," she teased. But she was serious, too. "I prefer to work in an environment with open communication, more give and take."

"Give and take?" He said the words as if he'd never put them together in the same sentence before.

"Yes. You're the employer and I'm the employee, but we discuss things and come to a consensus of what's best for the baby."

"A consensus?" It wasn't a question but a low voiced challenge.

"Right. You've made it clear you'd prefer to let the baby sleep in the morning while you escape to the sheriff's station. That's your side, and of course we could do that. But then there's my side."

"You have a side?"

"I do. I'm so glad you're getting into the spirit of things," she said through a smile, her tone carefully soft and easy; it was an attitude she maintained as she continued. "My side is I feel so strongly about your spending time with Carmichael that it's a deal-breaker for me. Either keep to the schedule we agreed on and have breakfast with him in the mornings, or you can find yourself another nanny."

The silence that followed screamed through the living room. Nikki dug her fingernails into the flesh of her palms to keep from squirming under his ferocious stare.

"I don't react well to threats, Ms. Rhodes."

"You know, I'm not really surprised to hear that." No understatement there. She lifted her chin and informed him, "I feel the same way about being blown off."

"Ms. Rhodes—" Ice encrusted her name.

"Mr. Oliver?" She gave chill as good as she got. He needed to know she was serious about this. "Think of it as the terms of my employment. And it's non-negotiable."

"It's a bluff. You said yourself you care about Carmichael."

"Which is why this is so important. I won't stand by and watch him decline further for lack of a steady influence in his life."

"You—"

"Stop." She held up a hand, palm out. "We've already established I won't be here for more than a few months. He needs the person who is going to be here that first day of school, when he learns to drive, and the day he turns eighteen. That, Mr. Oliver, is you."

Unable to dispute the truth, he stood silently glowering.

"Morning sessions with your son are the perfect opportunity to get to know each other better. Show him some attention and he'll love you unconditionally. It's pretty hard to mess that up."

"But what if I do? Mess it up?" he asked, with a concern that revealed a raw vulnerability his gruff attitude had concealed.

Her heart was wrung at the evidence of his fear of failing his son. She could think of no other reason why such a strong willed and private man would open himself to her. More than ever she renewed her vow to help father and son connect.

"I'll help you."

"The first thing you need to do is take off your shirt." Nikki opened a jar of baby food, poured the peaches into a bowl and set it on the table next to where Mickey sat sleepy-eyed in his highchair at the end of the table.

Out of near identical green eyes, Trace sent her a candid stare. "Must we go over the rules again, Ms. Rhodes?"

"Please. You have a one-track mind. I was thinking of your cleaning bill, not your manly form. You can take it off now or change it later. First lesson in feeding your child: babies are not neat."

"Thanks for the warning." Trace stripped off his khaki shirt and draped it over the back of the couch.

"Hey, I'm here to help." Nikki admired the snug fit of pristine white cotton stretched over wide shoulders when he returned to the dining area. She shook her head silently mourning the T-shirt's pending desecration. Oh, well, neat and tidy was an ongoing battle when you had kids.

"You take that side—" she waved Trace to a seat close to the highchair "—and I'll sit over here." They settled across from each other at the table on either side of Mickey.

"Okay, go ahead and give him a bite. Second lesson is never leave the baby unattended with the food, or you'll be cleaning the whole kitchen."

Trace took the bowl of puréed peaches, dipped the baby spoon in it and held it out to Mickey.

Mickey looked from the spoon to Trace, to her. He did not open his mouth.

"Move it closer," she encouraged Trace. "That's good," she said, when the spoon reached within an inch of Mickey's little mouth. "Sometimes you really have to shovel it in, but I'd rather he came to the food this first time between you."

Instead of going for the bite of peaches, the boy pushed away, leaning his head on the back of the highchair.

Huh? Nikki glanced over at Trace, to find him watching her with a "what now?" expression.

"Maybe he doesn't like peaches?" he offered.

"No. A lot of baby food is orange. Carrots, sweet potatoes, apricots—they make a whole guessing game of it at baby showers. I suppose if he didn't like one of those your mother-in-law may have catered to him and not fed him any orange foods. Did they leave a list of his preferences?"

"No. She wasn't in any shape to put anything like that together, and my father-in-law was too overwhelmed to think beyond dropping the baby off."

"Of course. That's understandable."

"There was nothing but formula and cereal in his diaper bag. There may have been some food in the refrigerator at my in-laws I could have picked up when I got his stuff last weekend, but I didn't think to look."

"She was still feeding him formula?"

"Yeah." He angled his head to the right. "There are several cans in the cupboard."

"If she still had him on formula maybe she hadn't even started him on baby food yet. Basic rule of thumb is formula for the first year, adding baby cereal at three or four months, and moving to baby food and other solids around seven to nine months."

Trace's jaw clenched and his eyebrows lowered in a grim scowl. Anger and shame flashed in his eyes, and she knew he blamed himself at this further evidence of his mother-in-law's smothering influence.

"Listen, those are just parameters. Like my sister says, there are as many theories as there are doctors. Mickey isn't suffering from malnutrition."

To distract him further, she scooted the empty bottle of peaches toward him. "There's baby food in the cupboard. Someone must have tried to feed him something more than cereal."

"That would be nanny number two. I arrived home one night at dinnertime. There was puke-green food all over him, all over her, all over the dining room. He was crying, she was screaming, and trying to force the spoon down his throat. I fired her on the spot."

Nikki chewed her bottom lip as she studied his stern expression. He'd obviously been appalled by the scene he'd walked in on. "That sounds very unpleasant."

"It was out of control."

Ah. The worst of all sins.

"Yes, well. I don't condone force-feeding, but you best prepare yourself. Feeding babies can be a chaotic experience. Most kids are naturally suspicious of any change in their diets. Some will easily try new things, but some need to have the food presented to them several times, and occasionally in different forms, before they take to it."

He frowned, as if it hurt to think about it, then he squared those truly impressive shoulders. "As I don't plan on lowering myself to Carmichael's level, I'm sure we'll manage just fine."

Oh, how the mighty would fall.

"A positive attitude is exactly the ticket," she assured him, figuring some things just needed to be experienced. "A smile helps, too. You know what they say— never let them see you sweat."

Trace lifted one dark brow. "We're talking about a baby here."

"Right." She looked down at her own white blouse and slid back in her chair. "Just remember they sense fear."

Trace grunted a nonverbal reply. Getting a good dollop on the end of the spoon, he presented the bite to Mickey once again. The boy wanted no part of it. He turned his head to the left, and when his father followed with the spoon he whipped his head to the right.

"Ack!" With a squawk of frustration, Mickey pushed Trace's hand away. A splatter of peaches flew through the air to land smack in the middle of Trace's chest. He glumly surveyed his formerly crisp white T-shirt.

"Good thing you took off your uniform shirt," she pointed out, hoping to direct him to the positive view. She got a grunt for her efforts.

His focus on the boy, Trace persevered, and finally got a good portion of the peaches into Mickey's mouth.

A tiny red tongue immediately pushed the food back out, then the baby blew a raspberry, spraying Trace with bright orange polka dots.

Nikki bit back a grin as father and son faced off, with identical frowns of stubborn resolve.

"You're the bigger man here," she reminded Trace, then giggled when they both turned those frowns her way. "You're not going to give up, are you?" she challenged.

"No." He narrowed his eyes at her, but she saw reluctant humor in the green depths before he turned his attention back to Mickey. "Okay, kid, no more spitting. Peaches are good, so open wide."

Before digging in for another bite, Trace licked a smear of peaches from where it had landed on his right thumb.

Mickey's eyes brightened, then he mimicked his father by licking his fist where he'd wiped the fruit from his mouth.

"Mmm, mmm." Nikki hummed yummy sounds and smiled encouragingly.

"Mmm," the boy repeated, and swiped his tongue over his hand again.

"Look." She grabbed Trace's arm and shook it in excitement. "Mickey's copying you. He likes it. Give him another bite."

Trace glanced up from where her hand rested on his arm. The heated stare he turned on her made her catch her breath. "No touching."

She snatched her hand away. "Seriously? You're in the middle of feeding your son!"

His gaze rolled over her, sensual as a caress, and so intense her skin tingled as if from actual contact.

He turned back to Mickey, feeding him another bite of fruit. "So? You've heard the statistics. The average man thinks about sex every so many seconds. If we aren't actually having sex, we're thinking about it."

Stunned nearly speechless, she leaned back in her chair and crossed her arms over her chest. "You dawg. And yet I'm the one who has to follow all the rules?"

The corner of his mouth twitched, but he came at her from a completely different direction.

"And, Ms. Rhodes? His name is Carmichael." He turned a reproachful stare on her, and she knew she'd slipped up more than once.

She grimaced. "I'm sorry."

She bit her lip, then decided to come clean. Truthfully, deception never came easily to her. Too often her mouth worked before her brain, and honesty just made life simpler.

"I just can't call him Carmichael. I promise it's not

meant to be disrespectful, or a control issue. Sure, Carmichael is a fine, distinguished name. But to me it's also cold and hard. And with all the changes in his life Mickey needs warmth and love and acceptance more than anything else. I'd constantly feel like I was scolding him."

Nikki got a first-hand lesson in Trace's interrogation technique as he sat back and ran a laser-sharp gaze over her. His intense regard seemed to see straight to her soul. He assessed, categorized and made conclusions—all without saying a word. Or changing expression. She was ready to spill her deepest, darkest secrets, and she had no idea what he was thinking at all.

He finally broke the connection to focus on mopping up his son's face.

Free to breathe again, she anxiously waited for his response. She hoped they could settle the issue amicably between them, because she really couldn't promise to call the baby Carmichael. In all honesty it probably wasn't harmful to the boy at this stage, but he'd responded to Mickey when he hadn't to the more formal name. That spoke volumes to her.

"Leslie Trace."

"What?" Nikki stared at her employer's stoic profile. Of everything he could have said, that made no sense to her. And when he turned to face her and flashed that dimple-popping grin she completely forgot what they were talking about.

"The name my mom used when I was in trouble." Humor and understanding had replaced the censure.

Evidently she'd hit the right mark, tapping into the universal connection of childhood memories.

"Leslie, huh? That had to hurt."

The humor disappeared. "Throw in extra for being a military brat. When my mom had gone, I told my dad I wanted to be Trace. He had no problem with that."

"Rough. How old were you when your mom died?"

"I didn't say she died. But she might as well have. I was ten when she left my dad and me."

"Extra rough. You and your dad must be close?"

"He died before I married Donna. But we weren't really close. Dad wasn't what you'd call demonstrative."

"That must be where you got it." As soon as the words escaped her mouth she knew she'd blown the moment.

Raw emotion flashed in his eyes before he shut down all signs of feeling. He rose to his feet and pushed in his chair in two short, controlled motions.

"Yeah, that's where I get it from." He glanced at Mickey before turning away. "I need to change."

"Trace." She jumped to her feet, but he was already gone. Slowly sinking into the seat, she met Mickey's confused frown. "Yeah, I know. I blew it."

CHAPTER FIVE

TRACE stared at the report on his desk as he waited on hold for the receptionist to make his appointment with the pediatrician. Finding out he didn't know the slightest thing about his son's health had struck Trace hard this morning. He'd depended on Fran to take care of Mickey and actually felt righteous about the decision. Fran and Owen had just lost their only daughter; they needed something—someone—to fill the void in their hearts and lives. Who better than their infant grandson?

How easy to convince himself the couple had been better suited to handle the newborn than an overworked homicide cop, with uncertain hours and no experience with living, breathing kids.

Sure, he'd made the effort to visit and provided monetary support. And, yeah, he'd made the move to Paradise Pines with the intent to take custody. But what it all boiled down to was he'd abandoned his son to a woman sick at heart over the loss of her own child.

He had no doubt Mickey had been loved and coddled. To within an inch of his life.

In retrospect he saw it so clearly. Fran had always had the baby in her arms or seated right next to her. Always insisted on feeding Mickey his bottle because it disturbed him to have anyone else do it.

She'd smothered his son with love to the point she'd stunted his development.

The return of the receptionist pulled his distracted attention from the report and his sorry history as a father. He quickly confirmed the appointment for Thursday at two and disconnected. Right. A microcosm of tension eased from the weight on his shoulders. He couldn't undo the past, but he could make sure they started out fresh, started out right.

He made a note to tell Nikki about the appointment.

Talk about fresh starts.

Trace was in serious trouble there. He didn't know whether he'd made the best decision of his life or a very dangerous mistake. Nikki Rhodes threatened everything he stood for: order, discipline and consistency.

Why, oh, why did she have to be exactly what his son needed most right now?

Trace kicked back in his office chair and stared unseeing out at the reception/dispatch area of the small sheriff's station. Instead of Lydia, his no-nonsense office manager, with a heart as soft as a marshmallow, he envisioned the soft golden beauty of his own personal Attila the Hun.

How had he lost control of his home so fast? His

home? Hell, his life. Mornings would never be the same again. Though he admitted to a proud moment when Mickey had taken his first bite of peaches from the spoon. What a sense of accomplishment. They'd grinned at each other, as euphoric as if they'd scored a winning touchdown and then—he cringed to remember this—they'd both turned to Nikki, as if seeking approval of a job well done.

She'd lavished them with praise. *Lord.*

Where was his self-discipline? Where was his pride?

He'd totally lost control. To a five-foot-five bit of fluff in a tight skirt and ruffles.

Okay, she'd thrown him off with her ultimatum, demanding his participation in feeding Mickey; he just needed to regroup and replan, set a new schedule. He admitted he'd been hesitant about spending time with the boy. But this morning's impromptu breakfast session proved he had nothing to fear. He could handle his son.

With a little tuition he'd become quite efficient. Then he'd send the distracting Ms. Rhodes on her way. They'd both be happier when she was teaching again.

For all her lack of structure, the woman had kept her promise to help. What had she said? "The benefit of open communication is you don't have to do everything alone." He had to admit he'd appreciated her assistance at breakfast. Sure he could handle it, but having someone there—it had been nice.

Another one of her precious gems of advice came to mind. "The good news is once you engage Mickey's affections it'll be almost impossible to lose it. Unconditional love is a powerful thing."

It sounded good. Too good to be true for a man who didn't know the first thing about love.

Nikki sat in one of her least-favorite places in the whole world: the doctor's office. One of the unsung joys of being a military brat was the military health service. Every new visit to the doctor brought a new face, and a new person to poke and prod you.

After the breakfast session the other day, she hadn't been surprised when Trace had insisted on a full checkup for Mickey. The idea that his son might have been suffering in any way drove Trace nuts.

She glanced at the little boy, quietly playing with blocks in his stroller. He was slight, but not noticeably undernourished. He might not have had a varied diet, but he'd had plenty. Still, the checkup couldn't hurt, and if it put Trace's mind at ease it might be worth this interminable torture.

"I'm only here for you." She leaned over Mickey. "And let's get one thing clear up front. I don't do needles—uh-uh, *nada*, no way. If there are shots involved, your daddy is on his own. In fact—" she flipped a block with her finger "—this is the perfect opportunity for father and son to go it alone. Yep, the two of you can bond over tongue depressors."

Mickey picked up the block to hand to her, but dropped it instead. He gave a small mew and shifted to look over the side of the stroller, then shifted his hopeful gaze to her. He looked so angelic, with his little bow mouth, baby-soft skin and windblown curls.

She handed him the fallen block and earned a smile. She sighed. "Okay, for you I can probably hang tough. But only if your dad asks for help. Otherwise I'm staying put."

"Daddy." He grinned.

"That's right. You and your dad are a team."

He went back to his blocks, and she returned to flipping leisurely through an entertainment magazine. She and three other women sat in navy short backed chairs. The walls and carpeting were beige on beige. An overflowing toy chest in the corner provided the only splash of brightness in the bland room.

The outside door opened and, like every other woman in the room with a sick child, looking for a distraction, Nikki glanced up. And, like every other woman in the room, her heart quickened at the sight of Trace. His broad-shouldered, narrow-hipped frame neatly filled the opening. His air of authority and control—elements he wore as easily as he did the crisp khaki uniform and gun belt—preceded him into the room. And shot up the temperature of every woman within viewing distance.

How unfair was it that the best-looking man in a fifty-mile radius had to be her boss? Not only did that put him both professionally and contractually off-limits, but the man was as disconnected from commitment as it was possible to be.

She sighed, and resigned herself to being his friend.

At least he was finally here, and they could get this appointment over with.

The clock over the receptionist's head read two-fifteen exactly. The perky blonde hopped to her feet, her bright smile aimed at Trace. "Sheriff Oliver? The doctor is ready to see Carmichael."

Wasn't that convenient? Nikki met Trace's gaze and slowly stood. The flash of panic, so unlike him, revealed a vulnerability she couldn't ignore. "Do you want me to go in with you?"

"Yes, please." He took control of the stroller and followed the nurse to an examination room.

Trace quickly expressed his concerns to Dr. Wilcox, sparing himself not at all.

An older man, with a ring of graying hair and wire-rimmed glasses, the doctor listened intently, nodding occasionally.

"Well, let's see what the real damage is." Dr. Wilcox smiled at Mickey, who scowled back at the man. With good reason. The doctor asked Nikki to strip the baby, and the poking and prodding began.

For a usually docile child, Mickey certainly made his displeasure known, twisting and turning so Nikki almost lost her grip on the boy.

"Here, let me have him." Trace stepped forward to trade places with her. He easily held the boy in place, but Mickey's distress only increased. He lifted his little arms toward Trace. "Daddy."

Trace's jaw clenched, but he stayed tough.

Thankfully, the doctor soon ended the exam. "Okay,

you can dress him." He picked up his chart. "Do you know what inoculations he's had?"

Nikki stepped forward to dress Mickey.

Trace reached in his pocket. "I went by my in-laws' place this morning and found a few things. This is a list of the immunizations he's had. I also called his pediatrician there, and asked for a copy of his file to be sent to you."

"Thanks. That'll be helpful." Dr. Wilcox looked over his glasses to scan the list Trace handed him. "And this looks current." He sat back and folded his arms over a barrel-size chest. "You can calm your concerns. Mickey is in good shape. The muscles in his legs are underdeveloped, which is consistent with your theory that he's been held a lot, but his bones are strong and there are no signs of malnutrition."

Nikki met Trace's gaze, and in that moment felt a sense of connection in their relief and gratitude at the doctor's news. Bouncing Mickey in her arms, she shot Trace a reassuring smile and let the tension drain away.

"Continue feeding him solids, and encourage him to use his muscles. I'll do the blood work and read through his records when they come in, then I'll give you a call. Basically, I don't expect I'll need to see him before his eighteen-month check-up."

"Thanks, Dr. Wilcox, that's good news."

"He's a precious gift, Sheriff," the doctor said seriously. "Treasure him accordingly."

Trace's cool gaze ran over Mickey, once again strapped in his stroller. "Right."

Nikki watched the exchange with little satisfaction. She'd so hoped something good would finally come from a visit to the doctor's office.

After a week of make do trips to the corner mini-market, Nikki finally dragged Trace to the grocery store on Saturday afternoon.

Pushing Mickey in one of the store carts, Nikki rolled over the threshold, and they both sighed at the rush of cold air.

"That's much better, isn't it?" She tweaked the boy's nose.

"Neeki." He grinned and made a grab for her nose, missing by a good eight inches.

She leaned closer and wiggled her nose. "Not going to get me," she challenged, and quickly pulled back when he tried again.

Mickey giggled, but next to her Trace frowned. "You're taunting a one-year-old?"

She simply smiled. "Oh, we've played this game before. He'll get me a couple of times before we're through."

Trace grunted. He looked at the aisles surrounding them, the people wandering nearby. "Let's get this done. I suggest we split up and meet at the register in twenty minutes."

Nikki sized him up. Cool and confident in jeans and a blue knit shirt, he clearly didn't want to be here. But it was more than the chore that had him off-stride. The man defined the term *loner*. In the week she'd been at the house she hadn't taken a single message for him. She knew he'd kept Mickey's existence to himself. Other than the doctor's appointment, this was his first public appearance with his son in the community.

Well, he needed to suck it up—because, in the way of small towns everywhere, everyone would soon know his business.

"You're out of almost everything, so we won't be out of here in twenty minutes. *And* you ducked out of breakfast yesterday, so you have Mickey-time to make up and this is the perfect opportunity. If we split up, he goes with you."

Trace shrugged. "Fine."

His easy compliance didn't fool Nikki. He was never comfortable handling Mickey alone. No one would know it, watching the two together. Though always gentle, always patient, Trace's need for control kept him from letting his feelings show, or he'd have already earned Mickey's love.

"Okay, then. He's going to want things he can't have, and touch everything within reach, so be firm and keep to the middle of the aisle."

"Really, Ms. Rhodes, I think I can handle a one-year-old in a store."

She lifted a skeptical brow. "That's what you said about feeding him the first time."

He planted his hands on his hips and met her stare for stare. "My point exactly."

Nikki cocked her head and considered him. Peach-stained T-shirt aside, she allowed that he'd persevered until Mickey ate the whole bowl. Since then he'd mastered the art of feeding the child without wearing half the food.

"You're right." But before Nikki stepped back and let him have the cart she needed to issue another warning. "There's one more thing—"

"Ms. Rhodes." He cut her off. "I can take it from here."

"But you should know—"

"We'll be fine." He took the list she held in her hand and tore it in two. "Meet you at the registers in twenty minutes."

Nikki shook her head and walked over to snag a new cart. Oh, well. She'd only meant to warn him that a man alone with a child in a grocery store was a total chick magnet. Actually, that was true anytime, anywhere, but in a grocery store it rose to the level of speed-dating. Or so a single dad had once told her.

But then maybe that was what Trace needed. To meet a few eligible ladies. He'd been a widower for nearly fourteen months. And he had Mickey to think about.

He was a smart man. He probably knew exactly what trolling the store with Mickey would bring.

The two of them deserved some happiness after the past year of hardship. She turned down the juice aisle. So why did the thought of another woman in their lives sting Nikki in the heart?

Five minutes later she saw Trace and Mickey start to roll past her row, but when Trace spied her he made a quick turn. He stopped next to her and without a word transferred the items in her cart to his, before stepping aside and waving her into the driver's seat.

She moved into position in front of Mickey, and assessed Trace out of the corner of her eye.

He crossed his arms over his chest and glared at her. "That was just mean."

"What?" She tried not to laugh at his disgruntled expression.

"Don't play innocent. It doesn't become you."

She grinned. "I did try to warn you."

"Yeah, well, next time I'm likely to be eaten alive by piranhas, make me listen."

She rounded the corner into the meat section. He selected steaks, while she picked up some chicken and pork chops. Moving on to the dairy section, she dared to broach the topic of his love life.

"So you're not interested in finding someone new to spend time with?"

He went still. "No."

She waited for more, but it became clear nothing further would follow. She pushed. "It's too soon? You must have really loved your wife."

He avoided her gaze by reaching for a block of cheddar cheese. "What I felt for my wife doesn't matter now. I need to focus on raising my son."

"Of course. But you shouldn't deny yourself a fulfilling relationship. A partner would be a benefit to Mickey, too."

"And why is it *you're* not married, Ms. Rhodes?" Those amazing green eyes swept the length of her and back up.

Heat flooded her cheeks. Those eyes exerted the most astonishing effect on her. As if he saw clear to her soul.

"I've had offers." But none worth giving up her freedom for.

"I'm sure you have," he acknowledged. "Yet you remain single. It's not a bad thing to know your own strengths and failings."

"True." And pretty deep. Had he gotten all that by looking into her eyes? Was her need for independence a strength or a failing?

Disconcerted, she turned down the next aisle and found herself facing an assortment of dog food.

Trace, following on her heels, asked, "Do we now have a pet I don't know about?"

She cleared her throat and continued down the lane. "Don't be silly."

"I don't know," he mused with wry humor, "you've wrought such change in my household anything is possible. I can easily see you thinking Mickey needs a companion, followed by a trip to the pound."

"I'd never do such a thing," she denied, her chin in the air. "Not without discussing it with you first."

He laughed outright. "Thanks for the concession."

"Hey, I'm not the one who'd be walking the dog in the middle of the night."

"I see how it is."

She grinned. "We'll just put the puppy discussion on hold for now."

"Agreed. Mickey takes all my attention."

"Hello! Hello, Sheriff Oliver. It's Mavis Day, from

the Historical Society." A tiny woman with a helmet of blue-gray hair in a bright pink shirt rolled up beside them. A white miniature poodle rode in the child's seat in a purple handbag.

"Of course. Mrs. Day," Trace greeted the woman. "How are you?"

"Suffering from the heat, like most of the population. My Pebbles just can't take these high temperatures. Just the thing to spend a bit of time in the cool of the grocery."

"We take our relief where we find it," he assured the woman with a polite smile. "No law against that."

"No law!" Mavis twittered. "Aren't you funny?"

"I make the occasional effort." He turned to introduce Nikki but stopped, and she saw his hesitation. It shouldn't, but that pause hurt.

Because he had his reasons, she smiled and prepared to move on. "Don't worry about me, obviously Mrs. Day has something to talk to you about. I'll be at the baby food."

He frowned.

"Oh, no, dear, you don't have to run off." Mrs. Day waved a wrinkled hand adorned by a truly impressive diamond. "I just wanted to thank you, Sheriff Oliver, for suggesting the pot-luck dinner for the community meeting next Wednesday. Such a thoughtful way of getting people involved in community affairs. But I didn't mean to disturb your time with your new lady-friend and her beautiful daughter."

Oh, my, a double whammy. Nikki sneaked a peak at

Trace, noted his narrowed eyes and the hard line of his mouth, but before he could correct the woman, Mrs. Day ran right on.

"I can't wait to tell the ladies at the Historical Society. I will admit I enjoy sharing happy gossip."

Trace turned sideways, so his profile faced the woman, before rolling his eyes. Nikki took that to mean Mrs. Day enjoyed sharing gossip of any kind. The accompanying impatience in his glance revealed his displeasure at being the topic of gossip at all.

"I'll tell you straight, we in the society have been worried about you. Many of us are or have been widows, and we know how hard it is to move on, to rejoin the dating pool. But it's been over a year—"

"Mrs. Day," Trace cut in, his voice a strangled growl.

"It's okay, Sheriff," she prattled on, patting his hand where it rested on the handlebar of the shopping cart. "It's important to accept that life goes on. There comes a time when you have to make a move, or miss your chance at future happiness."

A tickle in Nikki's gut forewarned her this conversation could not end well. Mrs. Day couldn't know the good Sheriff as well as she thought to make *that* pronouncement.

Mrs. Day nodded sagely. "If I hadn't grabbed him up, the Widow Thompson would have snagged my Mike. He's a good man. He does like those smelly cigars, but he steps out to smoke them. Does his farting out there, too." She turned to Nikki. "As you know, dear, a woman appreciates small considerations like that."

Nikki met Trace's stunned and appalled glance, and knew hers was equally bug-eyed. She bit her lip to keep from laughing out loud. The outrageous statement defied any other reaction.

"Mrs. Day, you have the wrong impression. This is my son, Carmichael, and his nanny, Nikki Rhodes."

Nikki liked the sound of her name on his lips. He continued to be formal with her. Though she called him Trace, and had asked him to call her by her first name, it was always Ms. Rhodes. She suspected he used the formality to foster distance between them.

"Oh." The woman blinked, and then smiled, waving her diamond again. "Your son. Of course. He's a charmer already. These lovely curls fooled me for a moment. And don't worry about the relationship thing. It'll happen. I have a feeling about you two."

This time Nikki didn't dare look at Trace at all. He seemed speechless. To add to the ridiculousness of the moment the poodle now popped up from the purple purse and yipped. Twice.

Mickey jumped, giggled then clapped.

"Shh, Pebbles." Mrs. Day quieted the dog as she glanced worriedly over her shoulder. "Mr. Wilson will hear you." She sent Trace a brazen grin. "I won't keep you any longer. I have to keep moving. Mr. Wilson and Pebbles have a love-hate relationship. She loves the cool air in here, and he hates the fact she's a dog. Oh, there's Millie. Did you hear her mother broke her leg? She was washing windows and fell off a stepladder. Her ma likes to have a cold cocktail on these hot afternoons. I hope she had more sense than to drink before climbing a ladder."

Mrs. Day tucked Pebbles back into her purple habitat and maneuvered her cart around Nikki's.

"I'll just go offer my commiserations."

"Take Pebbles home, Mrs. Day." Trace issued the warning in his official voice. "I wouldn't want to have to run you in because Pebbles and Mr. Wilson got into an altercation."

The woman waved away his advice. "You are so funny."

He watched Mrs. Day trot on to her next victim, then turned to Nikki with a lifted brow. "She thinks I'm joking."

Nope, Mrs. Day didn't know him well at all. Trace didn't joke about the law or keeping order.

"Lighten up, Sheriff," Nikki said. "You don't always have to chase the rules."

CHAPTER SIX

Trace tossed his keys on the counter and glanced at the clock on the kitchen wall: twelve-thirty in the morning. He headed straight through the house to Nikki's rooms to collect Mickey.

The whole town was buzzing about his business. Asking after his son—or, worse, his daughter. Wanting to know about his nanny service. Offering to set him up with their daughter, sister, niece and, in one unforgettable case, an ex-wife.

He just wanted it to end. Had never wanted it to start. But that had been unrealistic, and the hurt expression on Nikki's face when he'd failed to introduce her to Mrs. Day still haunted him.

He owed her an apology. It wasn't her fault his privacy was being torn to shreds. She deserved better from him.

He knocked once, and then again. After a few minutes Nikki opened the door. Hair mussed, dressed in shorts and tank top, displaying lots of silky soft skin. There'd been a couple of nights when he'd had to pick

Mickey up from here, but this was the latest he'd been. He'd obviously woken her.

"Hey," she said around a yawn, and stepped back. "You're late."

"Yeah. Sorry to ruin your day off."

"Couldn't be helped," she said easily. "Mickey was a big hit at my sister's baby birthing class."

He preferred not to imagine that scene. "I'll bet."

Backlit by the dim room, she looked sleepy, tousled and oh-so-soft. With a fierceness he'd never known, he longed to sweep her up, carry her to the couch and surround himself in her softness. He wanted nothing more than to purge the horrors of the night in the tenderness of her arms.

"Come in." She stepped back, and he moved past her to get Mickey from the playpen beside the couch. After hours of working at an accident, the sweet scent of her skin nearly drove him to his knees.

"The doctor called today. I gave him your cell number."

"Yeah, I talked to him."

"What did he have to say?" She crossed her arms over her chest.

Trace shook his head. It was too dangerous for him to be here. "We'll talk about it tomorrow."

He lifted the slight weight of his son into his arms. Mickey opened his eyes, focused on Trace, smiled and snuggled into his shoulder and went back to sleep.

The trust of the gesture weighed heavy on a night when he'd witnessed senseless death. How was he supposed to keep his child safe in a world out of control?

"Are you okay?" Nikki ran a light hand from the back of his elbow down his forearm to his wrist. Just as he'd thought, her gentle caress eased some of his despair.

To shatter the illusion he moved away, starting toward the door. "No touching." He tried for lightness and failed miserably.

The concern in Nikki's eyes heightened. She smiled. "This is my place. The rules don't apply here."

"The rules always apply." No rules meant anything went, and he'd have no reason not to taste the lush line of her lips. Soon he'd be looking for a new nanny.

She shook her head. "Not always. Did you eat? Why don't I put on some clothes and come heat up some food for you, and you can tell me what the doctor said?"

"I'm fine." Food sounded good, but more trouble than he wanted to go to this late. "I'm just going to shower and go to bed. Good night." He pulled the door closed and waited until he heard the bolt.

Ten minutes later he had Mickey tucked into bed, and was stepping from the shower when he heard a knock on the back door. It could only be Nikki. He considered ignoring it. Hadn't he faced enough temptation tonight? But he owed her for his previous rudeness.

Sighing, he pulled on a T-shirt and a pair of navy sweatpants and went to answer the summons. He opened the door to a steaming plate of food. Savory aromas floated to him on the night air, making his stomach growl.

Nikki cocked her head and grinned. "It goes against my civic duty to let the Sheriff go to bed hungry."

She'd donned low-riding gray sweatpants, and her pink tank top stopped just above her waist, leaving a band of creamy skin visible. The sight of her made him hungry for more than food.

"Is that macaroni and cheese?"

"It's homemade mac and cheese. Plus smoked sausage and sliced tomatoes."

"Okay, you can come in." He took the plate and left her to follow him. "How did you manage homemade macaroni and cheese with only a coffeemaker and a microwave?"

"It's leftovers from dinner with my sister. It's my mom's recipe. I make it better."

"This is pretty good." He stabbed a piece of sausage. "You'll have to send my compliments to your sister. It must have been rough on the two of you to lose them both together."

"Yeah." She sat down across from him and laid her hands flat on the table. "But they would have wanted it that way. My mother was a good military wife, she went wherever Dad was stationed. They loved each other very much—were the center of each other's lives. My sister and I completed the circle, but they always came first for each other."

"It must be nice to have had such a bedrock foundation."

"There were trade-offs. Mom coped with all the travel by micromanaging what she did have control of—the family."

She reached out, caught herself, and her fingertips

stopped just shy of his. How he resented that quarter-inch of space.

"It was bad tonight?" She zeroed in on what was bothering him.

"Two dead at the scene. A man fell asleep at the wheel. Killed himself and his adult daughter. The wife survived, but she'll just wish she were dead."

"Oh, Trace. I'm so sorry. It must be difficult to work accident scenes after losing your wife to a drunk driver."

"I had to leave Homicide. I couldn't make death my business anymore, or deal with it every day. This is better. There's probably the same amount of fatalities, but they're spaced further apart. And it's not the focus of what I do."

"No community meetings when you worked Homicide?"

The corner of his mouth lifted. She had a talent for making him smile. "Hardly. I was just asking myself how I'm supposed to keep Mickey safe in today's world. So much violence. Accidents, disease... Every couple of months there's an accident on the highway. With the casino on the reservation so close we see drunks, sleepy gamblers, tourists coming from the east. Illegal aliens freeze or die from the heat, trying to cross over the mountains. I'm all he has. What happens to him if something happens to me?"

"Trace, you know better. You can't focus on the negative. Make the most of what you have. Build your own bedrock with Mickey. Amanda and I knew we were loved, and that's huge—especially when there are a lot of changes or unknowns in your life."

Great. "And I'm the current unknown in my son's life."

"No, you're the new constant in his life."

"Little Miss Sunshine."

"Please." She rolled her eyes. "I'm more blunt than most people find comfortable. I'm working on my tact," she said with wry humor. "Tomorrow you'll feel better."

"Maybe." But he wouldn't be any less responsible for Mickey, wouldn't be any less alone. He pushed his empty plate away. "Excellent. Your civil servant thanks you."

She grinned, picked up the plate and carried it to the sink. "You know you're not alone." She took a glass from the cupboard, poured some milk and placed it in front of him. "Your in-laws are on the east coast, not dead."

"I think they've done enough damage."

"What about *your* parents? Would they be able to help you out?"

"Ha!" A harsh bark of laughter erupted from his throat. "My parents make Donna's look like parents of the year. At least they erred on the side of caring too much." Maybe the late hour had his defenses down, or maybe he was mellow after the warm meal, but Trace found himself talking to Nikki.

"My mom was the opposite of yours. She didn't want to follow Dad around, but he insisted. He wanted me with him. Don't know why. He wasn't a demonstrative man. Anyway, she'd had enough by the time I was ten, and she left us."

"Trace." Her soft heart overrode the rules and she covered his fingers with hers. "That's so sad—for you and your father. Was he in the military when she met him?"

Her touch warmed him more than her sympathy. Maybe that was why he'd opened up tonight. Because he'd known the tenderness she showed Mickey every day would be his reward.

"Yes. Within a year after leaving us she'd remarried and started a new family."

Her fingers tightened on his. "I hope you know she wasn't a victim. She knew your dad was military when she married him. *She* changed the rules on *him*."

"I learned all I know about emotions from my dad. She said he had no feelings and I was just like him. We weren't enough for her."

"She said you lacked emotion and then she abandoned you?" Nikki's shoulders went up and a fierce glint lit up her eyes, making them gleam like liquid gold. "Stupid woman."

He laughed. Something he wouldn't have thought possible tonight.

God, she made him feel good. Her humor, her compassion, her sheer willingness to go to battle for him turned his melancholy mood into something altogether different.

And altogether more dangerous.

"I like you, Ms. Rhodes." Again his attempt at lightness failed. The words came out husky, a growl of want.

The momentum of her emotions had pushed her forward over the table, so her weight rested on her elbows and their faces were mere inches apart. Eyeing the delicate curve of her mouth, the silky creaminess of her skin, he sought desperately for control.

Smiling sheepishly, she lifted her gaze from his mouth. As their eyes met, hers darkened, and she licked her lips.

"I like you, too, Sheriff Oliver," she whispered.

He watched the words form, her lips shiny with the essence of her, and longed to move the few inches necessary to taste her.

Instead he pushed away from the table, creating vital distance between them.

"You should go."

Nikki let herself in the back door. "Hey, it's just me," she called out, though she doubted Trace heard over the wails coming from down the hall. Still, she continued to speak as she went to investigate. "I need to pick up some laundry."

She stopped in the bathroom doorway. Ah, bathtime. Mickey did not like to be wet. The otherwise sweet and cheerful baby turned into a wild child whenever dipped in water. Throw in a hair-washing, like now, and he was one unhappy, slippery mess.

Trace was kneeling next to the tub on a bathmat, soaked from shoulders to knees. A drop of water fell from his hair to land on his cheek, disappearing into his five-o'clock shadow.

The Sheriff looked good wet. Nikki took new appreciation in why men liked wet T-shirt contests. Transparent cotton clung to his skin, defining hard muscles flexing in motion.

Enjoying the show a little too much, she knocked on the door. "Hey, what's all the ruckus about in here?"

"Save yourself. It's not safe in here." Trace only half looked over his shoulder, but it was enough for her to catch the frown of frustration and concentration furrowing his brow. "And it's a good thing he doesn't talk yet, because the language is pretty ripe."

"Neeki! Neeki!" At the sight of her Mickey renewed his efforts to reach safety, struggling in Trace's grasp and lifting his arms for her to rescue him.

"Stay still, you little eel," Trace said. "We just have to finish your hair and you can get out."

"Hang on." Nikki turned into Mickey's room across the hall.

Carrying a plastic blue puppy back to the bathroom, she could swear she heard him mutter, "Coward."

"I heard that, but lucky for you I'm going to save your hide anyway." She knelt next to Trace, glad she'd worn shorts.

"Oh, I'm lucky," he grumbled, keeping a hold of his slippery son so he didn't fall and crack his head. "Mickey, sit down."

Mickey's frown matched Trace's as he nailed him with a glare and yammered off a string of angry baby talk.

Nikki grinned. "I think it's a good thing we don't know what that means."

"Oh, we've had quite the conversation. I just need him to stay still long enough for me to rinse the shampoo out."

She wiggled her eyebrows at Trace. "Watch how it's

done. Hold him steady," she told him, and then, focusing on Mickey, she smiled. "Hey, baby, Daddy just doesn't know the trick, huh?" She brought the blue dog up and wagged it in front of the tearful Mickey. "He doesn't know Puppy gets his hair washed first."

Mickey quieted as Nikki swiped some bubbles up and worked them over the plastic blue head of the toy dog. Distracted, the boy reached for the toy and held it while Nikki made a show of washing the dog's hair. "That's the way," she encouraged Mickey. "We're washing Puppy's hair. And next it's your turn. Smile," she said to Trace, flashing her gaze over him. "That ferocious look probably works wonders with criminals. Not so much frightened little boys."

The frown instantly cleared. A light of humor even touched his green eyes. "Hey, you've got it backward. In case you didn't notice, the kid had the upper hand."

She laughed. "Hand me the small pitcher from the left-hand cupboard," she said quietly to Trace. He placed it in her hand, and she scooped up half a pitcher of water and poured it over Puppy.

Mickey squealed, and dunked Puppy in the water, splashing both Nikki and Trace.

"First dog food, now a puppy in the bath." Trace sent her a sidelong glance. "You're determined for me to get the boy a dog, aren't you?"

"Not guilty," she denied. "I always wanted a dog when I was a kid, but my mom said we weren't settled enough to make a good home for a dog, that it wouldn't be fair. She was right."

"So you're saying we aren't ready for a dog?"

"No." She refused to let him trip her up for his amusement, his own form of distraction. "You said you needed to focus on taking care of Mickey, and I agree with you."

"So no dog?" He grinned, proving she'd caught him in his game.

"Not yet. Good boy," she praised Mickey. "Time to do *your* hair. Close your eyes." She squeezed hers closed for a moment, to show him what she meant. He copied her, and she quickly dumped clear water over his head. He started to whimper. "Hang in there, big boy, only one more time." She made quick work of it, and Trace was right there with a fresh washcloth to dry Mickey's face.

"Nice job." Trace easily lifted Mickey from the water and Nikki wrapped him in a towel. "Thanks for the help."

"No problem." She shrugged easily. "We adults have to stick together."

"I thought you had a birthing class with your sister tonight. What are you doing here?"

"I do, but it's later—not until eight. I came to pick up some things I left hanging in the laundry room."

"In appreciation for the assistance, you're welcome to join us for dinner. It's only hot dogs and beans, but I'm firing up the grill."

"Thanks, but I can't. Amanda is stir-crazy, and since she has permission from her doctor for the classes, she's sneaking dinner in first and calling it all one trip. But it's a tempting offer."

More tempting than it should be. Plain food in the company of the baby she spent all day watching. Like Amanda, Nikki should be thrilled at an outing away from the house. Instead, she felt curiously deflated as she turned away from daddy and son.

"Okay," he said easily. "Thanks for the help."

"Good night." She grabbed her things from the dryer and let herself out the backdoor. Was it her imagination, or had he sounded a little disappointed?

CHAPTER SEVEN

"THE Mayor's office called." Lydia popped her head inside the door to his office. "He's asked the city council to meet at Sampson Hall twenty minutes before the community meeting."

Trace nodded, glanced at the clock on the wall, saw he had over an hour and went back to his report. He'd found it hard to concentrate today, his thoughts constantly traveling back to the scene a couple of nights ago. He'd come close to getting extremely unprofessional with his nanny.

He so couldn't go there.

Mickey needed her. Beyond that she was a complication Trace couldn't afford.

The door to the station opened and in walked the subject of his thoughts. She pushed Mickey in his stroller, with a long, shallow basket perched on the hood over the boy's head.

Everything in Trace came to attention, his body reacting to the long stretch of her legs in skinny black jeans, the teasing pop of a pink tank at the hem and the cleavage under her fitted white shirt even as his mind raced with questions and concern at her appearance.

What was she doing here?

He rose and rounded his desk, watching her chat and laugh with Lydia. Her easy manner eliminated his worry, but not his disquiet.

He shrugged at the tension in his shoulders. He didn't want her here. This place belonged to him—well, and the citizens of Paradise Pines. The point was he needed someplace safe as a retreat from her intoxicating presence. But, no, interfering woman that she was, she had to invade his workspace.

Oh, yeah, he was in serious trouble.

As soon as he stepped out of his office he got hit with the savory scent of fried chicken, which reminded him of the potluck dinner at tonight's community meeting. He had an order of fried chicken himself, to pick up from the diner. The scent grew stronger as he approached the front counter, but he was quickly distracted by the tail-end of Nikki's introductions.

"It's so nice to put a face with a name. It's always good to know when Trace is going to be late. Have you met Trace's son, Mickey?"

Lydia had her elbows on the high counter to help her see down to Mickey's level. The little boy looked up at her with solemn eyes. He switched his gaze to Trace, frowned, and then twisted in his seat, obviously seeking out Nikki's reassuring presence.

She casually moved to the side of the stroller, giving

him a clear view of her, and Mickey settled back into his seat. At the same time she moved the cloth-covered basket to the counter.

"Hey," she greeted Trace, her dimple flashing as she smiled.

"Trace, your nanny just introduced me to your son. I never heard you had a child. All this time I've chattered away about my grandkids and you never mentioned you had a little boy." Lydia's teasing reprimand held more than a hint of hurt. "He's so precious."

Damn, moments like this were exactly why he liked to keep his private life separate from his public service. Personal exchanges required too many complex twists of emotional discourse. So what if he suffered occasional bouts of loneliness? He preferred things simple.

"Thanks. He's only been with me a short time. His grandmother has been caring for him while I got settled." Trace hated to explain himself, to expose his personal life, but it was that or subject himself and Mickey to the gossip mill for civic entertainment. That he couldn't tolerate.

"Well and fine. I bet you've missed him every day." Lydia gave a sympathetic nod.

"It's been hard," Trace acknowledged, "but we're together now." He focused his attention on his wayward nanny. "Ms. Rhodes, I wasn't expecting you."

"They called from the diner to say your order was ready." She lifted the red gingham napkin, revealing two dozen pieces of fried chicken. "Mickey and I were looking for something to do, so we decided to save you a trip and pick it up."

It looked as good as it smelled. Her homey touch adding to the presentation. Who knew he even owned a gingham napkin?

"You didn't need to do that," he informed her.

"I know." She glanced at Lydia and shrugged. "He's the perfect boss. He never wants me to go out of my way for him."

"You're a nanny, not a housekeeper." Again with the explanations. How much easier if she'd stayed at home.

Not once had Donna come to visit him at work, and he never remembered his mom dropping in on his dad. Of course if she'd ever shown more interest in what the old man did, got him talking about it, maybe he would have found it easier to express himself at other times. And if his dad had been better at communication maybe his son would be, too.

"Don't worry, there's no extra charge." Nikki waved off his clarification. Instead she grinned and gave an exaggerated look around. "All it's going to cost you is a tour of the place. I've never been in a sheriff's station before. Do you have cells here?"

"We have a couple of holding cells." Now, there was a thought. Maybe one of those could hold her long enough to give him a few minutes' peace. He took control of the stroller and started toward the back hall. "Grab the chicken. We'll begin with my office."

"Don't forget your meeting with the Mayor and the city council before the community meeting starts," Lydia called after them. He waved an acknowledgment.

For someone who always seemed to move at a slow

glide, Nikki easily kept pace. "I really do want a tour, but if you don't have time I understand. I know the meeting starts in an hour. We can do this another time if you like."

What he'd like was her pressed up against his office wall, with the door shut and the blinds closed…

He almost tripped over his own feet as the scene played out in his head.

"Are you okay?" she asked when he came to a dead stop.

"Yeah, fine." Holy heck, where had that come from? "On second thought—" he made a U-turn away from his office "—let's put the chicken in the kitchen."

The illicit vision was wrong on so many levels, yet so vivid he practically tasted her on his lips.

He was the Sheriff, this was his office, she was his employee. And those were only the obvious objections. He had a son to worry about—a son who needed her more than Trace needed his libido ignited.

If none of that existed he *still* wouldn't act on the crazy desire. She was all about love and commitment, and he'd already proved he knew next to nothing about those commodities.

"Have you always wanted to be a cop?" Nikki asked Trace as they neared the end of the impromptu tour. Pride in what he did showed in every word he said as he took her through the small station. She'd been booked, fingerprinted and was about to be processed.

"I was military first. Marine, like my dad. But I decided I liked having more control over my life, so I only did four years. Law enforcement seemed a natural choice from there."

"Structure and discipline on your own terms?"

He watched her out of the corner of his eyes, obviously bothered at being pegged so accurately in a casual observation. Actually, he'd surprised her. She hadn't expected him to be so at ease, so funny. This was where he felt at home.

"As a teacher of twenty to thirty five-year-olds, I'd think *you'd* be a fan of a controlled environment," he challenged her.

She laughed. "What I know, as the teacher of thirty kindergarteners, is that control is an illusion."

"Come on, you give me a schedule for Mickey every day. You have routine down to a science."

"Oh, I'm all about structure and routine," she readily agreed—those were a teacher's biggest tools. But his version and hers were polar opposites. "But in the classroom my day moves from one chaotic moment to the next. When you work with kids you have to be flexible. You never know what's going to happen, so you have to be prepared for anything. I imagine your days are much the same."

He shook his head in disbelief. "You're comparing a kindergarten class with criminals?"

"Of course not," she assured him. "But keeping the peace, monitoring behavior, dealing with cultural differences. It's all part of our day."

"I never really thought of it that way."

"Most people don't, but a classroom is a microcosm of the community. Oh!" She spotted a stack of thick books full of photos. "Are these mugshots? Can I look?"

"Yeah, they're older versions, hard copies. Most mugshots are online now. Technology is great. It helps to narrow down by characteristics—height, weight, coloring, etcetera. But sorry." Trace walked to the counter holding the books and flipped the covers closed. "The pictures are for case purposes only." He shrugged. "Every one gets their privacy protected these days. Even known felons."

"Actually, I can understand that." Nikki fingered the edge of one of the books. "I check the public Web site for sex offenders on a fairly regular basis. And I can tell some people are only there because of indiscretions gone public."

"Let me guess." He stood hands on hips, every inch the hardcore cop. "You think it's unfair for a dumb college prank like mooning someone in a passing car to classify someone as a sex offender?"

"No," she disagreed—surprising him, no doubt. She drew in a calming breath and tried very hard not to think beyond the conversation. "It's a hard line, but if someone is stupid enough to expose themselves in public then it could be a precursor of future deviant acts. When it comes to the safety of kids, I don't think the line can be too hard."

Needing the distraction, and a reminder of all things innocent and good in life, she checked on Mickey. He slept peacefully in his stroller, his thick lashes a dark shadow on baby-soft skin. His sweetness helped settle the ghosts of harsh memories.

When she stood up straight, Trace was too close.

"I'm sorry," he said gently.

"What?"

"You've dealt with a victim of sexual abuse?"

She swallowed hard. Obviously she hadn't been as good at hiding her feelings as she'd hoped. "It was the hardest thing I've ever had to stomach in my life. The helplessness was overwhelming."

"Nikki." He cupped her cheek, his thumb a soft caress as he swept away a tear. "You have to know you helped."

"Too little, too late." For just a moment she rested her head on his shoulder, absorbed his strength and his warmth. "She was so small, so quiet, how could anyone want to hurt her?"

His fingers laced through her hair as he hugged her to him, his touch tender where his body was all hard muscle. And his low voice whispered to her. "There's no sense to be found in these cases. You help where you can and live with what you can't change."

She shook as memories bombarded her. "I've never known such hate. I can't think about it or I lose myself in the rage."

"No," he agreed, "you can't dwell on the bad." He lifted her chin so she looked into his intense green gaze, so close she could see the scars on his soul, and she knew he knew. "You have to focus on the good you did. You can't let the hate win or she won't be the only victim."

"That's what the counselor said. And most of the

time I can deal with it. Monitoring the public Web site gives me a sense of being proactive. Being responsible for young kids is huge, and I want to be able to protect them when they're in my care. If I can recognize a predator before he harms a child, it's worth the effort."

"I think you're brilliant. Now, what can we do to put a smile back on your face?" He eased away, but his hand warmed the small of her back, holding her steady. "Do you want to see how my handcuffs work?"

"No," she mumbled, as she took the tissue he handed her. As she mopped her face and his heat retreated, she realized what an emotional mess she'd become. How mortifying. Trace must want to be anywhere but here right now. But as she peeked at him around the tissue he looked anything but terrorized.

"Nikki," he said. Her name. Nothing more. But the softness of it, the intimacy of it, broke down the distance his persistent formality upheld between them.

Even as her mind shouted *bad idea*, Trace stepped close again, lowered his head, and claimed her mouth. On a catch of breath, she opened to him, and he deepened the kiss. A hard arm around her waist swept her closer to him, so they touched from shoulder to thighs, his strength and confidence an intoxicating combination as she melted in his arms.

Ignoring the warnings clamoring through her head, she surrendered to the passion, meeting his tongue with hers in a sliding dance of desire.

It felt so good to be held, to lean—just for a moment—on someone strong and giving.

She drew back at the thought, recognizing despite her passion-drenched senses the fallacy of her conception. She had no right to lean on Trace. This was a moment out of time for her. For him.

She had no doubts he'd be as appalled as she once they regained their equilibrium. Stepping back, she cleared her throat, seeking a less-dangerous distraction.

He'd been wonderful, actually. It had really helped to talk to someone who understood. But time to let him off the hook.

She lowered the tissue and batted her eyes at him. "I don't think I'm ready for handcuffs, but you can let me shoot your gun."

His gaze blazed a molten emerald heat. It took him a moment to move from hot and bothered to cool, calm lawman. Blinking, he cleared his eyes and propped his hands on his gun belt. He narrowed his eyes at her. "You want to shoot my gun?"

"Yes, please."

He shifted his gaze from her to the sleeping baby then back. "Now you're just pushing my buttons. This isn't the time or place for target practice."

"Okay, yeah, a little." She cleared the thickness from her throat and tossed the tissue into a nearby trashcan. "But maybe we could go to the range sometime."

"Guns aren't toys, you know." He looked so torn— all macho cop, but still wanting to distract her from her emotional meltdown. How sweet was that?

"Actually, I do know. My dad was a navy chief. He taught me to shoot. We used to go to the range together."

The Reader Service — Here's how it works:

Accepting your 2 free books and 2 free gifts (gifts valued at approximately $10.00) places you under no obligation to buy anything. You may keep the books and gifts and return the shipping statement marked "cancel". If you do not cancel, about a month later we'll send you 6 additional books and bill you just $3.84 each for the regular-print edition or $4.34 each for the larger-print edition in the U.S. or $4.24 each for the regular-print edition or $4.99 each for the larger-print edition in Canada. That is a savings of at least 15% off the cover price. It's quite a bargain! Shipping and handling is just 50¢ per book in the U.S. and 75¢ per book in Canada.* You may cancel at any time, but if you choose to continue, every month we'll send you 6 more books, which you may either purchase at the discount price or return to us and cancel your subscription.

*Terms and prices subject to change without notice. Prices do not include applicable taxes. Sales tax applicable in N.Y. Canadian residents will be charged applicable provincial taxes and GST. Offer not valid in Quebec. Credit or debit balances in a customer's account(s) may be offset by any other outstanding balance owed by or to the customer. Please allow 4 to 6 weeks for delivery. Offer available while quantities last. All orders subject to approval.

NO POSTAGE
NECESSARY
IF MAILED
IN THE
UNITED STATES

BUSINESS REPLY MAIL
FIRST-CLASS MAIL   PERMIT NO. 717   BUFFALO, NY

POSTAGE WILL BE PAID BY ADDRESSEE

THE READER SERVICE
PO BOX 1867
BUFFALO NY 14240-9952

If offer card is missing write to: The Reader Service, P.O. Box 1867, Buffalo NY 14240-1867 or visit www.ReaderService.com

"Really?" Clearly surprised, he swept his emerald gaze over her with a new level of interest that had her breath catching in the back of her throat.

"Well, then, it's a date."

"He asked you on a date?" Amanda's fierce whisper shouted her amazement. "I knew having a hot boss was going to be trouble. What'd you say?"

"No need to get so agitated." Nikki shushed her sister. "It wasn't really a question. And no definite plans were made. Thank goodness. I told you the agency forbids romantic interaction between nannies and clients. I don't want to lose this job when you have less than a month before you're due."

With a disgusted toss of her head, Amanda settled back in her metal folding chair. "No fair, teasing the pregnant lady."

They were seated on the aisle at the back of Sampson Hall, waiting for the community meeting to start. Mickey still slept in his stroller. After her visit with Trace, and their shared moment together, Nikki had walked across the park, needing the quiet stroll to gather her composure.

The kiss and Trace's mention of a date had thrown her heart into turmoil. These past weeks she'd tried so hard to keep her professionalism wrapped around her, to keep his strength and vulnerability from getting to her.

"Hey, you're supposed to be talking sense to me, not seeking vicarious thrills." Okay, Nikki would *not* be sharing news of the kiss with her sister. She needed

Amanda to help bolster her resistance, not encourage her to pursue the enemy. Mickey had already stolen her heart; she couldn't afford to give any of it away to Trace. That way led straight to heartache.

"My husband is gone again, after being away for five months, and I'm the size of an elephant." Amanda patted her swollen belly with love and resignation. "I'll take my thrills where I can find them."

Nikki shot Amanda an aggravated frown. "Not at my expense. You're not even supposed to be here."

"I didn't want to miss the meeting, and I'm just sitting. Come on, just give me a few details. I need something to keep my mind off the ticking clock. I can't believe how much I want this over at the same time as I'm dreading labor and the birth."

Nikki squeezed her sister's hand. "You're going to do fine."

"I'd do better if Dan were here."

Hearing the tears in Amanda's voice, Nikki gave in. Amanda needed distracting, and Nikki needed to talk. It was also a reminder of how vulnerable Amanda was, how much she needed Nikki to stay close. Which meant no more stolen kisses with the boss.

"Okay, the truth is I asked him out."

"What?" Amanda squealed, causing Mickey to flinch in his sleep. "What about the agency rules? I thought you were determined to keep your distance."

Nikki rubbed Mickey's belly until he settled. "I was. I am. It's just keeping my objectivity is harder than I anticipated."

"Duh. The man is gorgeous."

"He's also intelligent, brave, dedicated and caring, though he tries hard to hide the last one."

A furrow marred Amanda's brows as her concerned gaze met Nikki's. "You're falling for him. Oh, babe, you have to stop."

"Don't be ridiculous."

"I know you and your soft heart. These two are getting to you. Why else would you ask Trace out?"

Nikki waved a dismissive hand. "It wasn't like that. We were in the middle of a heavy moment. I just wanted to distract him."

"By asking him on a date? Are you out of your mind?" Amanda shifted in the uncomfortable chair. "What was the heavy moment about?"

Nikki explained about the tour and the difficult discussion, carefully playing down the part where she'd fallen apart in his arms. "He was trying so hard to make me feel better. I just needed to change the subject."

"So you asked him out?"

"I told him I wanted to shoot his gun."

Amanda just stared at Nikki, slowly shaking her head. "Tell me you're joking."

It was Nikki's turn to shake her head.

"He could interpret that in so many ways!"

"Amanda." Nikki stopped her. "It wasn't like that." Oh, God, it had been exactly like that. "Nothing is going to come of it, so there's no reason to rehash the whole thing."

"I thought you needed me to talk you down from the edge."

"Let's say you scared me straight and call it done. I'm going to get us some food. Stay put and keep an eye on Mickey." Grateful for a chance to escape, Nikki slipped from her seat.

"Mickey wants chocolate cake," Amanda said hopefully.

"Yeah, right. Mickey's playing hooky, and his doctor said he needed to control his weight over the last month." Leaving her sister muttering about mean doctors, Nikki headed to the back of the room toward the buffet table.

A small cluster of women had gathered near the end of the table.

"I'd do it, but I promised several people I'd address the land issue," a slender blond woman said.

"Yeah, I'm supposed to take notes for my neighbor because she had to work late," plump redhead added. "I have her toddler and mine. I was hoping to put both kids in childcare."

"I wish Cindy had let us know sooner she wouldn't be here." The owner of the diner planted her hands on her hips and looked over the crowd.

"We all want to hear about the Anderson endowment. I just know the men are going to want to use the land for another sports park, when this is the perfect opportunity to bring a little culture to Paradise Pines."

"What about your niece, Sarah? Can she come down and babysit?" the blonde asked.

The redhead shook her head. "She's working at the theater in El Cajon this summer."

Nikki stepped forward. "Perhaps I can help. I don't mind watching the kids during the meeting."

As one, the three women turned hopeful gazes toward her.

Trace stood in the corner, his gaze alert on the crowd, talking to a couple of local businessmen. All conversation stopped when Nikki appeared next to his group.

"Gentlemen." She acknowledged the men with one sweeping smile as she handed a plate of food and a cup of punch to Trace. "Carry on," she advised, as she turned on her heels and returned to the buffet.

As preoccupied as she'd been in her hit-and-run delivery of the plate in his hand, there was no way she'd gone unnoticed by the men he'd been talking to.

Sure enough, Trace pulled his glance away from her to find the two men silent, their gazes locked onto Nikki's black-and-white curves.

"Hmm. Why do *you* rate the special treatment?" asked Cord Sullivan, Mayor and owner of the local nursery.

Trace sent his friend a quelling glare.

"So that's the nanny? Nice," said Parker, the local barber, who was loud and coarse by nature. His eyes on Nikki's retreating rear end, the rotund barber was oblivious to Trace's displeasure.

"Get your mind out of the gutter, Parker." Trace sent him a killer stare. "She's my employee."

"Yeah, that's a sweet setup you have going."

Trace invaded the man's space. "What did you say?"

Parker nearly swallowed his tongue to keep another

suggestive comment behind his teeth. He blinked and backed up a step. Maybe the man had more sense than Trace had given him credit for. "Hey, I'm just saying she's fine." Parker looked after Nikki again. "If you're not interested, maybe I'll give her a call."

Over Trace's dead body. As if Nikki would give the older man a second glance. She was all sassy honesty, and Parker was brash and oily.

"Don't bother," Trace said, his tone hard, his posture stiff.

"Right." Parker nodded and winked. "Message received."

Trace shook his head, but didn't correct the man. Better that he think Trace and Nikki were involved. That way, the fool would leave her alone.

Not that Trace was jealous.

He had no right to that emotion.

It's a date… The words echoed through his head and he wondered again what he'd been thinking.

And that amazing kiss.

Now, *there* was evidence he'd hadn't been thinking with his mind. He couldn't remember the last time his body had held sway over his head. Maybe being sex-starved and lonely had finally taken its toll, making him delusional.

Nikki had completely absorbed his thoughts during the brief meeting with the city council. Thankfully he'd known what the Mayor was announcing, or he'd have been clueless going into the meeting.

He could not date his nanny. More, he'd be a fool to

date Nikki Rhodes. No way he could live up to her emotional standards.

Look what had happened the last time he'd let loneliness direct his actions. He'd ended up with a strained marriage, a son he didn't know and a hot piece of fluff living in his garage.

Okay, that was harsh. But he needed to stay real and he had no business admiring the strength and fortitude hidden under frivolous ruffles and lace. Besides, they were totally incompatible. She liked to chat and he wanted silence. She had big-time control issues and he liked to be in charge. She loved kids and he couldn't even relate to his own son.

Bottom line: he had nothing in common with the loving and dedicated Ms. Rhodes.

Hell, if Donna had lived Trace had no doubt they would have ended up another divorce statistic. Just like his mom and his old man.

Best he forget he'd ever mentioned a date.

Besides, she probably wouldn't even be around to accept an invitation. If a teaching job came along she'd be off and on her way, leaving him and Mickey to pick up the pieces of their lives without her.

No—wait. That had been his mother.

Oh, yeah, serious trouble. In spades. It was not a good thing when he was comparing his nanny to his long-lost mother.

CHAPTER EIGHT

"HEY, little boy, we're home." Nikki parked the stroller on the front deck, unstrapped Mickey and lifted him up. "Are you ready for a snack? I'm ready for a cold drink."

She unlocked the door and stepped inside. As usual she went to set the diaper bag on the sofa, and just stopped herself from dropping it on Trace. He lay stretched out on his back, fast asleep.

"Oops," she whispered. "Daddy's taking a nap."

Trace home in the middle of the day was far from usual.

Still in his uniform, including gun belt, he looked as if he'd come in, sat down and crashed.

"Daddy night-night?"

"Shh, yes—Daddy is sleeping." Not wanting to disturb Trace, she took Mickey to the kitchen and put him in his highchair with some grapes. A glance at the clock on the microwave showed she and Mickey had been away just over an hour. How long had Trace been here? And how long could he stay?

Checking to make sure Mickey was okay, she picked

up the phone and called the Sheriff's station. After Lydia answered, Nikki explained the situation.

"I just wanted to make sure he doesn't have any appointments or anything I might need to wake him for," she finished.

"Let me check his schedule." Lydia went away and Garth Brooks sang about the rodeo. "He has a meeting, but I'll call and reschedule for tomorrow. Let him sleep. He's had a couple of late nights."

"Yeah, it was after eleven when he brought Mickey to me last night. I kept the baby for the rest of the night, so I don't know what time he got home."

"It was a bad scene last night. Domestic disturbance. Trace went with the wife and kids to the hospital, then saw them settled in a shelter. Husband will do jail time if she follows through with pressing charges."

"Tough night." How many times had Nikki already said that to Trace? She admired him for his courage and fortitude. His wasn't an easy job, but a necessary one, and he handled it with calm efficiency.

"Tough job." Lydia echoed Nikki's thoughts. "Tell him to forget about coming in unless I call him. I'll get the guys to split his shift. He deserves the rest."

"I'll tell him," Nikki answered dryly. "But I make no promises."

Lydia laughed. "I wouldn't expect you to. The man does have a stubborn streak."

"Do tell. Duty is his life."

"But life doesn't have to be all duty." With that cryptic message Lydia hung up.

Did she mean duty didn't always have to be a heavy load? That the lighter side of responsibility was companionship and caring?

Nikki bet Trace didn't see it that way. Now that father and son were well acquainted—they didn't run the other way when they saw each other coming—it was time they started enjoying each other's company.

"Daddy! Daddy!" Finished with his snack, Mickey banged his empty bowl on the highchair tray and called out for his father.

"Shh." Nikki shushed the boy again, and quickly snagged the bowl away from him. "Daddy is sleeping. And it's time for you to take a nap, too." She wiped his hands and face. "That'll give me time to figure out an activity for the both of you for tonight."

"Night-night?" he said, a scowl forming on his tiny features.

"It's daytime, so just a nap."

"No," he protested, even while a little fist rubbed his eyes.

"Yes, Mickey is a sleepy boy."

"Boo?" He asked after his favorite stuffed animal.

"Yep, it's Boo's naptime, too." Nikki settled Mickey and his stuffed giraffe, Boo, down, and then put in a load of laundry. While she puttered and cleaned, she plotted.

A barbecue might be just the thing. The boys could cook the meat while she put together a salad or dessert. Humming, she took out a couple of steaks to thaw.

* * *

Something soft and damp landed on Trace's cheek, then slid toward the corner of his mouth. He opened one eye and found Mickey in his walker, right next to the couch.

"Hey, buddy." Trace yawned. The kid was cute, but the curls had to go. He made a mental note for Nikki to schedule a trip to the barbershop.

Mickey flashed his four-toothed grin and patted Trace's cheek again. "Daddy night-night?"

Trace stretched and glanced at the window. He hadn't slept that late, had he? No, the sun still shone, but the shadows indicated he'd slept longer than he'd intended.

"Nope just a nap." He sat up and scrubbed his hands over his face. "Now Daddy has to go back to work."

"No, no." Mickey jumped up and down in the walker, stood still, and then jumped some more. "No, no."

"Good boy, work those muscles." Some of the anxiety Trace had held on to since the visit to the doctor's office eased. In the past couple of weeks the boy had grown visibly stronger.

Trace glanced at his watch and groaned. "Great. I missed my appointment with the principal."

"No, Lydia rescheduled you for tomorrow," Nikki said from behind him.

Frowning, he turned so he saw her. She stood at the kitchen table. She pulled one of his T-shirts from a laundry basket, folded it, and set the shirt in a pile on a clean towel she had laid out on the table.

"How do you know that?"

"You were dead to the world when we got back. I didn't want to wake you unless you had something scheduled so I called Lydia. She said it had been quiet today and to let you sleep, and that you shouldn't bother coming in unless she called you. She was going to get some of the guys to cover for you."

"Huh, the woman thinks she runs the station. Late nights come with the territory. I can handle it."

"The point is you don't have to. Lydia juggled the schedule." She hit him with a knowing look. "You're just afraid the guys will think you're weak because you came home for a nap."

"I didn't come for a nap. I brought home a file last night to go through before my meeting today and I forgot it this morning."

The corner of her mouth twitched. "Which means you came in, sat down and conked out. I think that says something."

Picking up a couple of plastic blocks from the floor, he placed them on the tray of Mickey's walker. The boy immediately grabbed one in each hand and clapped them together.

When she was right, she was right. Deciding to drop an argument he couldn't win, Trace addressed a new issue. "I told you not to bother doing my laundry."

"I'm not doing your laundry. I'm doing Mickey's laundry," she said, as she shook out another extra-large T-shirt, crisply folded it and set it on top of two others.

"Either those are my shirts, or you're dating a man named Mickey."

She grinned. "They are your shirts. But I only threw

them in because I needed to fill up the load. You wouldn't want me to waste important resources, would you?"

"You always have an answer, don't you?"

Standing, he rubbed a hand over Mickey's downy soft hair. He was now trying to eat the blocks. Trace maneuvered the walker into the middle of the room, giving Mickey space to move around. He immediately pushed himself back three inches. Backward was his main directional pull. He still needed to master forward.

"I am a teacher. I'm supposed to have the answers."

Trace hid a chuckle in a cough. Not wise to encourage the woman. She already challenged his authority at every curve. But she did make him laugh.

"And the towels?" He fingered the stack next to his shirts.

She shrugged. "I love the feel and smell of a warm towel fresh from the dryer. It's a small delight. I didn't think you'd mind."

"Liar."

"Moi?" she asked, all innocence. "Not about this."

"You're spoiling me, Ms. Rhodes." Loose gold tendrils curled over her ears, and he fought the desire to test the sunshine softness. "And I like it too much."

Her eyes flashed. "I think we're past the Ms. Rhodes stage, don't you?"

"I think it's prudent."

"And I think it's too late for that."

"You mean, because of the kiss?" Of course because

of the kiss. The taste of her, the feel of her in his arms, still haunted him.

"Yeah." She met his gaze, then looked away, checking on Mickey in the living room. And Little Miss Ostrich surprised him when she asked, "You want to talk about it?"

"Absolutely not. I'm doing my best to forget it ever happened."

That earned him a coy glance from under dark lashes. "How's that working for you?"

"It's not. But it's prudent."

"Hmm." She seemed to consider his diversionary tactics. "I thought you believed in confronting issues head-on."

"Well, Teach, I'm learning new things from you all the time." He grinned when she rolled her eyes.

She continued to tuck and fold, and he sighed. Maybe she'd brought it up for reasons of her own. "Do *you* want to talk about the kiss?"

Her brow furrowed while she thought over his question. The myriad of emotions in her amazing golden eyes matched much of what he felt: confusion, attraction, regret and more.

"Yes," she finally allowed. But she chewed her lip, not saying anything further, obviously struggling for the right words.

Feeling defensive, he assured her, "You don't have to worry. I promise it won't happen again."

Her gaze on his mouth, half wistful, she nodded. "It can't happen again. It's more than just professional ethics, it's written right into my contract. And I have to stay close to Amanda in case she needs me. I can't risk losing this job."

"Of course." The tension in his shoulders eased as he realized she hadn't found his kiss objectionable. It was the situation she stressed over. He shouldn't care, as the kiss wouldn't be repeated, but somehow he did.

"There's Mickey to think of, too," she added, concern evident in her earnest expression. "He may get confused by a change in our relationship. He's making such good progress we don't want to do anything to jeopardize his growth."

"You're probably right."

"It's prudent." With a small smile, she echoed his earlier assurance. "There is something else I'd like to talk to you about. If you're not going back to work, I thought you might grill some steaks and we could eat out on the deck and talk."

"I should go back." He checked his watch, saw there was only an hour left of his scheduled time. He'd put in a lot of extra hours lately, so he could justify the time off. And sitting down to a meal and conversation with Nikki sounded really good. All the more reason he should get his butt to work.

"Let me check in with Lydia. If it's still quiet, I'll stay and grill."

"Great." She smiled her pleasure. "I'll get these clothes put away and start on a salad." Stacking baby shirts on top of baby pants, she headed toward Mickey's room.

Trace sat on the couch to make his call. He met his son's gaze across the room. "Whatever you do, don't leave us alone tonight."

Every day her attraction for the handsome Sheriff grew stronger. The sooner father and son connected and she could move on the better. For them. And for her. Nikki watched through the kitchen window as the boys "grilled."

Trace had changed into a sky-blue polo shirt that emphasized the width of his shoulders, and a pair of khaki shorts that came to his knees but left his muscular calves on display. He made one fine view.

While he wielded the spatula, he instructed Mickey on the finer points of barbecuing. Mickey listened and chewed on a teething biscuit.

Male bonding at its best. Just as she'd planned. Not scheduled was the joy she took in the family moment.

For a man who held himself aloof, who claimed to have no capacity for emotion, he was amazingly insightful and compassionate. Nikki suspected it wasn't that Trace didn't acknowledge his feelings, it was that he felt things so deeply, and if he allowed himself to feel he couldn't do the work he did without being torn apart inside.

He looked up and met her gaze through the window. He smiled, and butterflies fluttered in her stomach. Not a good sign.

"Steaks are ready," he called.

She waved an acknowledgment, gathered the baked potatoes and salad bowl and joined the boys outside.

Under the shade of the umbrella the summer air felt warm against her skin, but the breeze gave the evening a balmy feel.

"This is nice." Trace set the platter of steaks on the table. "Good idea."

Easy conversation followed while they ate. She found out they shared a taste for action movies and biographies, but couldn't be further apart when it came to music and Chinese food. His growing sense of humor delighted her.

They talked briefly about the big announcement made at the community meeting. Nikki had been babysitting the kids, but her sister had filled her in on the Anderson endowment, gifting funds and property to Paradise Pines for community development.

"Is it true the men already have plans drawn up for a new sports complex?"

"It's no more aggressive than the women hiring an architect for a museum."

"Please. The cultural significance of a museum over a sports park couldn't be more blatant."

"Kids want to go to the park. They have to be made to go to a museum."

"That doesn't make the need for culture any less important in their development."

"So you're siding with the women?" Even he heard the sarcasm in the question.

She gave him an arch stare. "I am a woman, and I help shape young minds as a living. I can't believe you don't see the value of learning over play."

"Statistics show kids in team sports are more socially adept and less likely to get involved in drugs, alcohol and gangs. I see the value in that."

"Yes, but we already have a sports park. We don't have a museum." Already seeing the argument forming on his lips, she cut herself short. "Never mind. We have to work together. It's best we accept we're on opposite sides of this issue."

"Good idea. Too bad the whole town can't agree to disagree. I see this getting ugly before it's over."

"Keeping the peace." She grinned at him. "That's why you get the big bucks."

"Ha, ha. The big bucks came from my dad's life-insurance policy. And I inherited my wife's trust fund that she got from her maternal grandmother. I didn't want any of it."

Wow. The emotional outburst was so unlike him she stumbled for a response. "It must have helped, though, to allow you to make the move to Paradise Pines and to buy this place."

His fist tightened around his glass. "I can afford to provide a home for my son."

Okay, that hadn't been the right thing at all. Stupid, in fact, with his pride all wrapped up with his loss.

"That's not what I meant. I'm just saying that money isn't intended to replace the people we've lost but to help us adjust to life without them. My mother insisted on life-insurance policies for both her and my dad. Without it neither my sister nor I would have been able to complete college."

"That's different."

"Why? Because we were college-age girls alone in the world instead of a big he-man like you?" She shook her finger at him. "Not only is that sexist, it's disrespectful to the dead. People get peace of mind in life and in passing to know the ones they love will be taken care of when they're gone. I'm sure you've already considered what arrangements you're going to make for Mickey."

He drew a circle on the table in the condensation dripping off his glass of iced tea, conveniently avoiding eye contact. "I already moved his mother's trust fund into his name."

Of course he had. "See? I bet she'd be pleased with the gesture."

"Yeah." Mickey dropped his sippy cup and Trace bent to retrieve it. When he settled back in his seat, tension showed in the tight line of his shoulders. "How is it you can read me so well?"

"I listen," she said lightly, offsetting the near accusation with an airy response. "My mom always said it was a gift. I have a talent for hearing people. She felt it would help me to be a good teacher. And you're not so hard to read." Her bluntness got the better of her. "You're an honorable man, who puts duty above all else."

He gave a sharp nod, as if agreeing with the assessment.

She should stop, she knew it, but something drove her on. She wanted to know more about him, and these odd moments of exposure offered an opening she couldn't resist.

"You want to know what I really see? From little things you've said, I get the feeling your marriage had begun to falter. But it kills you that you weren't able to protect your wife, to somehow keep her safe from the perils of the world that stole her life. Having a child wasn't your idea, and you don't love Mickey, but he's your son, so you'll do right by him and protect him no matter what."

"You can stop now." With an explosion of muscle he pushed to his feet and began to pace. "How can you know all that?" he demanded, his tone cold enough to frost the July night. "Have you been snooping through my things?"

"No. Of course not." Offended, and hurt by the accusation, she recoiled in her seat, crossing her arms over her chest. "You know I'd never invade your privacy in such a way."

"What I know is you're talking about things that are none of your business." He scrubbed a hand over the back of his neck. "I never talk about my wife. How could you have heard anything to make your deductions?"

She rubbed her arms, unprepared for his fierceness. "You're right. We should stop this."

She glanced at Mickey, to see how he was reacting to the sudden tension. Thankfully he'd fallen asleep, his little head resting on his arm stretched out over the tray. "I should take Mickey in."

"No." Trace reclaimed his seat, scraped the chair closer and propped both elbows on the table. "Answer the question."

This had gone too far. He was upset. She'd wanted to learn more about him, maybe rile him a little, but not to this extent. "Trace, I'm sorry."

"I don't want an apology. I want an answer."

"I really think we should end this."

"Nikki."

"Okay. It's not what you say, but what you don't say. You never talk about your wife except in relation to Mickey. And then you don't call her your wife; it's always 'Mickey's mother' or sometimes her name."

"I'm a private man. I don't talk about myself. That doesn't mean anything."

"No, but people who have lost a loved one generally do talk about them. It's a way to keep them with us even though they're gone. It's okay, you know," she said softly. "You don't have to pretend to feelings you don't have."

He sat back and crossed his arms over his chest.

"Don't tell me what to feel."

"And don't yell at me because you don't like what you're hearing. I'm right, aren't I? Or close enough to count. Otherwise you'd be laughing off my comments as so much fluff."

"I think it's time you left."

"You say you don't do emotions. Wrong. You seethe with emotions. You just don't want to deal with them, so you bury them deep down inside. You didn't love your wife—big deal. It happens. You feel guilty for her death. Not your fault. Get over it."

"Good night, Ms. Rhodes."

Chin up, her heart heavy, she reached for the dishes to carry them inside. "I'll come back for Mickey."

"Leave the dishes. Leave him. Just go."

Oh, she'd go. But not before putting in a fighting shot for Mickey.

"Emotions aren't something you're good at or not. It's just what you feel. How you act on those feelings is what makes the difference. If you can't find a way to open your heart to this sweet boy, he's the one who will suffer."

He made no response, but his eyes had changed from ice crystals to smoldering emerald heat. Good, let him brood.

Fighting off tears, she swept through the French doors to the kitchen, moving quickly toward the back door and the safety of her own rooms.

She stopped midflight, making a sudden decision to escape to the comfort of her sister's company. Let him work for it if he needed her in the middle of the night. Still, she should tell him. She was, as it were, on the clock.

He stood exactly as she'd left him, his stare focused on the dirty dishes littering the table.

She remained on the threshold. "I'm going to spend the night at my sister's. You can reach me there if you need me."

He didn't move, didn't even look at her. "I won't."

Why did the words cut her to the core? "Of course not. You don't need anyone."

Turning on her heels, she left him to his lonely existence.

CHAPTER NINE

TRACE pulled the SUV into his driveway, then reached for the large bag stuffed with sub sandwiches, fruits and salads. He felt foolish, planning a surprise outing, but now he'd moved into the execution phase he settled into action mode. The agenda for the evening flashed through his head.

Pick up food: check.
Fill cooler with ice, sodas and juice: check.
Pack blanket to sit on: check.
Persuade Nikki to accompany him and Mickey to the park: pending.
Apologize for being a jackass: two days overdue.

In those two days Nikki had barely spoken to him. She came after he fed Mickey in the morning, and left as soon as Trace got home in the evening.

He missed her.

Missed her cheerful morning chatter and her pretty

smile as she wished him a good day. Missed her company at the dinner table where she kept Mickey occupied while Trace ate. Missed the way she listened to him talk about his day and how her eyes lit up when they laughed over the crazy things people did.

He hadn't realized how easily she'd slipped past his guard until she wasn't around anymore. He wanted his friend back.

He owed her the apology. Two of the things he admired most about her were her blunt honesty and her insightfulness. How irrational of him to get angry with her when she turned those qualities on him.

She'd been right, and her dead-on accuracy had put him on the defensive. He'd felt exposed, and raw with emotions he couldn't identify. Guilt, fear, inadequacy, anger and more, until his pride had exploded, causing him to send her away.

Time helped him see the discussion more clearly, helped him see she'd been trying to help him.

Using his key, he let himself in the house. A quietness lay over the empty rooms, yet the place smelled great, of chocolate and vanilla, as if she'd baked. Anticipation built. If she were in the mood to bake, his chances had just gone up. He set the bag on the dining table and went in search of his fam—

He cut the renegade thought short. Nikki wasn't family. Yeah, he wanted to kiss her again, touch her, hold her, make her his. But it wouldn't happen, couldn't happen. Mickey liked her, and Trace needed her for Mickey too much to risk messing it up by getting cozy with her. Pending apology case in point.

No, it was best they stay friends.

Now, if his libido got on board, he might just make that work. When he reached the hall, he heard murmurs coming from Mickey's room.

He stepped to the doorway and looked in. Nikki stood over Mickey at the changing table. She'd obviously just changed him, and they were having a deep conversation about him keeping his hands to himself.

"Now, listen, mister, just because I have to lean over you to change your diapers does not mean you get to pull my hair." She poked him in the belly. "You keep your hands to yourself, buster."

Imagining his own hand fisted in her curls, holding her captive for his mouth, made Trace a little jealous of his kid. He didn't blame Mickey for using any opportunity to get his hands on those soft and lustrous tresses.

"Hey," Trace said, not wanting to startle her.

She turned to glance at him over her shoulder. For a moment her features lit up at the sight of him, and then she remembered her irritation and her expression closed up.

"Hello," she responded softly.

Another good sign. A man knew where he stood with Nikki. When she had a mad on she was all cold tones and go-to-hell glances—*after* she'd told you what a dork you were being.

Donna had locked herself away and sulked, and half the time he hadn't even known why. Was it any wonder he'd given up trying?

"Daddy, Daddy." Mickey's legs twisted and bucked as he tried to sit up, and Nikki fought to finish the changing job.

Trace moved closer, hoping the boy would settle down if he could see him.

"Hold still, you little octopus." She deftly pushed little legs into tiny blue jeans and pulled them up over his butt. "There, all done." She threw up her hands, as if finished tying off a steer.

Mickey rolled into a seated position and grinned at Trace. His little arms popped into the air—a bid for Trace to pick him up. Trace hesitated only a moment before lifting Mickey. The boy immediately wrapped little arms around Trace's neck and laid his head on Trace's shoulder. Trace patted his back.

"Is he sleepy?"

"No. He's just happy to see you."

"Oh. Good." He jiggled the baby, as he'd seen her do. "I was wondering if you had plans tonight?"

She eyed him warily. "I can watch Mickey."

"Actually, we'd like you to join us on an outing to the park."

"You're taking Mickey to the park?" A hopeful note mingled with surprise.

"Yeah." He nodded toward the kitchen. "I have a picnic meal and everything."

"Hmm." She considered him, and then left the room. He followed her down the hall and to the dining room table, where she peeked into the picnic bag. "Sandwiches, apples and grapes, pasta salad." She turned her head and swept him with a speculative glance. "A nice assortment of goodies, but you're missing dessert."

Moving to the counter next to the stove, she picked up a foil-covered platter. Bringing it to him, she lifted the corner to reveal chocolate-chip cookies. "Perhaps these will work?"

Her playfulness drew him forward. But he stopped short of reaching for her as he wanted to. Instead he bent to smell the cookies.

Looking up at her, he grinned. "Perfect."

Nikki leaned back on her hands and sighed. It didn't get much better than this: a mild summer evening, a soft place on the grass, and a view of father and son feeding ducks at the edge of the pond.

Trace handed Mickey some breadcrumbs and the boy threw them into the water, where five colorful ducks fought over the soggy meal. Mickey giggled and clapped and the whole process repeated.

She had their meal spread over the red gingham tablecloth Trace had included. They could have sat at a picnic table, but Trace wanted the full picnic experience. And Mickey had more freedom to move around on the ground.

"Dinner's ready," she called out.

Trace waved, and a moment later joined her on the makeshift blanket. "This looks great."

"You put it together. I just laid it out."

"Yeah, all my favorites." He settled Mickey between them and put a bib on him.

"Let's give him a few grapes to start out, and I'll feed him after we've eaten."

"Good idea." He took a big bite of ham and turkey sandwich.

She went for the pasta salad and some apple slices and watched him eat. She owed him an apology, and it was going to take more than the chocolate-chip cookies to salvage her conscience.

She didn't know where the conversation had gone so wrong the other night, but she knew it was her fault. Her bluntness landed her in awkward moments. When would she learn the virtue of tact?

Trace deserved his privacy, to grieve in his own way, to make peace with himself, or not, in his own time.

"I'm sorry." The apology came out strong and crisp, the sincerity clearly evident.

But it didn't come from her.

Trace met her gaze over the napkin he used to wipe his mouth. "You were trying to help and I jumped all over you. It was uncalled for, and I hope you can forgive me."

"Only if you forgive me first. I had no right—"

"Stop right there. Never apologize for caring. Not to me, not to anyone." His vehemence startled Mickey, and the boy's chin wobbled until Nikki smiled and tickled his cheek. Mickey grinned and popped a grape in his mouth, happy again.

"Being in the military, in law enforcement, I've seen more situations than you can believe that would have been cured simply if someone had cared." He peered into her eyes until she had to blink to escape the intensity in his. "From the beginning, I've told you things I've never spoken to anyone about. It's because it's there in your beautiful eyes—a genuine sense of caring."

He thought her eyes were beautiful. "Trace, I'm not some rare creature. Lots of people care."

"You're more rare than you think. Look at Mickey." They both focused on the baby, who'd snagged a cookie while they'd been talking and was smeared with chocolate from eyebrows to chin.

Nikki groaned. Now, there was the picture she wanted her boss to see right when he was telling her how attentive she was. Oh, well.

"Kiddo, you're a mess." She leaned over and kissed a clean spot on his cheek. "But you taste good. I might just eat you up." He giggled, and she laughed with him.

Gathering him into her lap, she looked around for the diaper bag. Once she'd located the bag, she found the wipes. "Sorry about that. I'll have him cleaned up in a snap."

Trace took the wet wipe from her and went to work on Mickey's face himself. Mickey giggled and wiggled, trying to dodge his father's efforts. Trace met her gaze over the boy's head. "This is what I'm talking about. A month ago he wouldn't have even touched the cookie, and now look at the fun he's having. He was despondent and sad and now he's happy."

"You have as much to do with Mickey's transformation as I do."

"Not nearly."

"You're wrong. He recognizes he's safe with you. Your steadfastness and the routine you've set give him necessary boundaries. He's thriving in the environment you've created."

"I wish I believed that."

"You can. Before you know it he'll be challenging those boundaries, but that's okay, too. In fact, it's great, because it means he trusts you."

Doubt played over his features as he leaned back on his hands and kicked his long legs out in front himself. "I still say you're the miracle-worker here. Mickey adores you. I'm totally second string."

"Not true." The man needed some strokes. "Mickey isn't the only one that's come a long way in a month. You've made strides, as well." She gently touched his fingers where they lay on the blanket. "He loves you, Trace."

A flash of longing crossed his features before he shut down all emotion. Such a strong, self-assured man. His lack of faith in himself broke her heart.

"I'll prove it," she said, and turned to face him on the blanket. "We'll put Mickey in the middle and let him choose who he goes to."

Lifting Mickey from her lap, setting him at the top of the blanket facing the two of them, she prayed this worked. She believed Mickey loved Trace, but he also cared for her. The truth was he could go either way.

She scooted back a few inches as Trace moved into position opposite her. He rested his hands on his knees and looked at her. "It's all right if he goes to you."

Mickey sat plump and happy at the edge of the cloth. He looked at her. She smiled and subtly nodded toward Trace. Mickey took the hint and turned his green gaze on his dad.

Yes. Relieved and excited, Nikki held her breath. He was going to choose Trace.

But he didn't. Back and forth went his little head. A frown began to pucker. Uh-oh.

"It's okay, baby boy." She softly reassured him.

"Hey." Trace shook a finger at her. "No trying to sway him from the sidelines."

Rolling her eyes, she said, "You are such a guy."

The scrutiny he leveled on her was all male. "Never doubt it."

Fat chance of that, she thought, feeling the potency of him shiver through her. She never forgot he was man to her woman.

At that moment Mickey rolled to his knees. Nikki tensed, urging him with her mind to crawl to his father.

He didn't.

But he didn't come her way, either.

He headed straight down the center, toward the chocolate-chip cookies.

"Oh, no, you don't." Trace swooped Mickey up.

Nikki laughed. "Look at that. He's already a diplomat."

"That's my boy."

Standing in front of Trace, Mickey immediately started in on his new favorite thing, jumping. Pumping and pushing, he squealed in joy. With his new diet he'd put on some weight and become quite the handful, yet Trace handled him easily.

"Well, there's no doubt you're his favorite right now."

"Yeah. It's good to see him thriving." He looked at her over Mickey's head. "Thank you."

"Hey, we're a team."

Trace went statue-still. Even Mickey stopped and looked at her. "I like the sound of that," Trace said.

Mickey put his hand out toward Nikki and she reached for him, but before they connected he suddenly broke away from Trace and took a step toward Nikki.

"Trace, look," she whispered, to keep from spooking the baby. "He's walking." She pulled her hand back a couple of inches, enticing him to take a couple more steps. He rushed those steps and fell into her arms. "Oh, my God, Trace. Did you see that? He walked.

"Oh, aren't you smart? Come here, you." Thrilled with his cleverness, she rained kisses all over his face. He grabbed her hair and hung on, giggling infectiously.

"He's brilliant." Trace clapped his hands, making Mickey laugh and clap, too. "Let's see if he'll do it again."

"All right." She grinned at Trace, and the pride and wonder on his face made her breath catch. She turned Mickey around and put him on his feet.

"Go to Daddy."

She wondered if he'd try to crawl again, but he didn't even hesitate. Hands flailing to help with his balance, he took off walking. He crossed the two-feet distance between her and Trace in a stumbling rush that almost ended in a fall, but Trace caught him and pulled him close.

"We're in for it now." Trace kissed Mickey on the top of his head and praised him lavishly. "If the way he took to the walker is any indication, we're going to be running to catch up with him from now on out."

Tears burned at the back of her eyes. This was the first time she'd seen Trace display more than casual physical affection for his son. Little pats and an occasional rub of his head were the usual for him. It seemed to be the day for baby steps.

"I'm so glad you were here for his first steps," she said, looking away from the pride in his eyes. Silently she groaned, because she had just realized Mickey might not have fallen, but she had. She was falling hard for Mickey's dad. And she might never recover.

How funny was that? A free spirit falling for a control freak. Not exactly a match made in heaven.

"You're right," she whispered. "Life will never be the same again."

"Sit down," Trace invited the next evening. He set his plate of spaghetti on the table and pulled out a chair. "You can tell me what you've been wanting to talk to me about."

"Oh." Suddenly nervous about her news, Nikki decided it might be better to catch him later, when he was fresher and not just home from a long day at work. "You're tired. We can talk about it tomorrow."

Her nerves must have shown, because he nailed her with a stare. "We've already put it off several times. You've mellowed me out with spaghetti and meatballs, one of my all-time favorites. The timing doesn't get much better than this."

Uh-oh. She was in real trouble if he started reading her mind.

Summoning a reassuring smile, she jumped into the deep end. "The day after the town meeting the community center received news that their pre-school teacher was quitting. Without notice. They asked me if I'd be interested in the job."

He stabbed a meatball, delivered the bite to his mouth, and chewed, assessing her all the while. Finally he pointed his fork at her. "You have a job."

"Yes, and I explained to them that Mickey would be my first priority. They have no problem with me bringing him to the classes."

Sitting back, he crossed his arms over his wide chest. "One child's not enough for you?"

Okay this was good. He was resistant but willing to talk. She'd expected less; she'd expected an outright decree to stay home with the baby. Not that he was a chauvinist, but he *was* a control freak. And a bit of a traditionalist. Funny, she actually liked that about him.

"I love Mickey. You know that. And this isn't babysitting; that's separate. These would be actual pre-kindergarten classes, two sessions a day, three days a week. Monday, Wednesday and Friday, nine to eleven and one to three, except there's no afternoon session on Fridays."

"So it's only fifteen hours a week?"

"That's not bad, right? I told them I was looking for something full-time." He scowled at the reminder. "And they said that wasn't a problem, they'd take me for as long as they could have me."

"It sounds like you really want to do this."

"I do." A true grin surfaced. Maybe he wouldn't object after all. "They were desperate, so I agreed to do a test session. I taught the afternoon class today. It reminded me how much I really love teaching."

"You miss it a lot?" He dug into his spaghetti again.

The question made her stop and think. Wow, surprisingly, the answer was she hadn't missed teaching as much as she'd thought she would. She'd enjoyed getting back in the classroom, but taking care of Mickey, sharing time with Trace, brought her a satisfaction that more than equaled what she got from teaching. Unsettled by the revelation, she refocused her attention.

"Yes," she admitted. "These kids were younger than I'm used to, so that presented some challenges, but they're so eager to learn. They absorb knowledge like little sponges."

"So you had fun?" He took a sip of milk.

"I did. If you don't mind, I'd like to take the job. Mickey would be with me most of the time, but now he's started walking, if he gets antsy they said he could go over to the daily care center with other toddlers and play there. It's just across the hall."

"Okay." He nodded. "As long as Mickey's taken care of, I'm fine with it."

Hot after a trip into town running errands, Nikki let herself into the house. Her little refrigerator didn't have a freezer, so she'd stashed some ice cream bars in Trace's.

"Knock, knock," she called, to announce her presence.

No answer. And a pungent smell hung in the air.

She knew they were home; she'd seen his SUV in the drive. On a whim, she grabbed a second bar and went in search of her guys.

She stopped, her heart flinching at the errant thought. Her guys. For now, but not for the long haul. The end of her two months was approaching. Trace no longer avoided his son. She really needed to give thought to saving herself from deeper heartache.

Maybe she'd be better off starting to distance herself from them. It was her day off; she had no real reason to see them.

The infectious sound of Mickey's giggle floated down the hall, stealing her willpower. She followed the sound to his room.

She stepped through the door to his room to find Mickey standing in his crib, throwing toys on the floor.

"If you keep tossing those out, you're not going to have anything to play with," Trace said over his shoulder, his attention on what he was doing. "I'm not coming over there again."

And, oh my, what Trace was doing. Here was the explanation for the smell. Paint. Light blue and bold primary colors, all on the wall facing the crib.

Trace was painting Mickey's room.

The blue was a background for a wall-filling mural

of Mickey Mouse and friends. Mickey stood, arms crossed, cocky in a leather jacket, scarf and flying goggles, while his Disney buddies formed a posse behind him, each character wielding sports gear. Donald Duck cocked a bat over his shoulder, Goofy twirled a basketball on one finger, while Minnie simpered over a tennis racket.

"Oh, my God," Nikki breathed, awed by the authentic quality of the drawing. Even half-finished, the colors popped and the characters brought life to the formerly dull room. "This is fabulous."

Trace turned at the sound of her voice. "Hey," he said, his vivid green eyes rolling over her from toenails to hair band, reminding her she'd been in his arms only days before. Then he blinked and stepped back to survey his work. "It's not turning out too bad."

"Not too bad? It wonderful. Did you draw this freehand? Since this morning?"

"Yeah, I doodle a lot. It passed the time on stakeouts and such over the years."

"This is more than doodling." She walked closer, studying the details. "This is art. You're very talented."

"I've never done anything this big before. So, you like it?"

"I love it. Mickey is going to love it." She handed him the second ice cream cone. "What made you choose Disney?"

Paint-stained fingers tore the paper off the treat. He nodded toward Mickey, who stood in his crib looking down at his toys. "I thought of sports themes, but I didn't want to pigeonhole him so young. This seemed like a good choice."

"It's perfect." She tossed her ice cream stick in the trash. "I'd love to see your sketches sometime."

He threw back his head and laughed. He looked relaxed and happy. Not a look he wore very often. "You did not just say that."

Replaying her words, she flushed, but couldn't regret her come-hither comment. It was the truth—in fact and in suggestive inplication. Even if she did need to keep her hands to herself.

"Probably against the rules, huh?"

"Big-time."

"But I really want to see them."

"Maybe some other time." He tossed his own ice cream stick. "I need to finish this."

"I guess you do." She watched as he went back to brushing color on the wall. Who knew he had this creative side? Proof of a sensitive side she'd long guessed he kept well hidden.

"Whew. The paint fumes are pretty strong in here. Is it safe for Mickey?"

"Yeah. I got the kind that's safe for kids and pregnant women."

"Good." She should have known. He was always careful with the details. She bent to pick up the dropped toys and return them to the crib. "Here you go, baby. Can I help?" she asked Trace.

"It's your day off. You should be out having fun."

"That's later—a barbecue at Amanda's. I can give you an hour."

"I won't turn it down. Can you wield a hammer?"

"With the best of them. My dad was a do-it-your-selfer and I liked to help."

"Great. There's a shelf and a mobile that need to go up."

"I'm your woman."

He sent her an ach glance out of vivid green eyes, but only nodded to the boxes piled on the dressing table. "Thanks."

"It'll be fun." She gathered hammer and nails from the garage and got to work. The mobile went up first, with Mickey watching every move she made.

"Looks good," Trace said. "Your dad taught you well."

"He did. I was a real daddy's girl."

"From what you've told me your family was close?"

"Yeah." She carefully marked her level points. "When you move around a lot you have to count on each other. Dad always found time to spend with us, or allowed us to be with him. He was great."

"You said your mom controlled the family. You two probably crossed swords a lot."

"Not when I was younger and we were traveling around. She was strict, yeah. We weren't allowed to join team sports or spend the night at friends' houses. Amanda and I learned to rely on each other and we grew very close. Mom—" Nikki swallowed around a sudden lump in her throat. She started over. "I realize now she was trying to protect us from being hurt, from making friends and having to leave them behind."

"Good intentions can sometimes have disastrous results," he sympathized.

"She did mean well." Anger, loss, and guilt had Nikki spinning to confront him, her defense of her mom quick and sharp. "Don't make assumptions about something you know nothing about."

He slowly turned, until Mickey's mouse ears framed his head, but it was the compassion in his eyes that she reacted to.

"She was a wonderful mom. Just because your mother abandoned you, don't be making judgments on mine. She did what she did because she loved us!"

"Nikki." He set the paint pallet aside to come to her. He cupped the side of her face, gently running his thumb over her cheek, wiping away a tear. "I'm sorry. Of course she loved you."

His understanding only made her feel worse, because she'd believed the same for the last years of her mom's life.

"No, I'm sorry—so sorry. I should never have said that about your mother. We did fight," she admitted around a strangled breath. "My mother and me. Once I turned eighteen and got to college I found a freedom I'd never known, and suddenly I blamed her for every restriction she ever enforced throughout my childhood."

"Don't be so hard on yourself. It's a normal rite of childhood to rebel at some point."

"But I understand now. I just needed more time with her. But she died instead."

"You said it yourself, Nikki. She loved you, and she knew you loved her, that's all that matters."

"No." She laid her forehead on his shoulder so she didn't have to look at him when she confessed, "The last time I saw her she was trying to give me some advice. I didn't want to hear it. We argued. I left mad." Anguish tightened the constriction in her throat so her voice became a husky rasp. "It was awful. And that's my last memory of her."

"Wrong." His fingers ran through her hair in soft strokes, his touch soothing her. "That's one of many memories you have. No matter how many disagreements you had, your mother loved you, and she knew you loved her. That's what you need to hold on to."

"Right. You're right. I have lots of memories." She lifted her head to meet his perceptive gaze. "Thank you."

He lowered his head and lightly touched his mouth to hers. "You're welcome."

Nikki grabbed the hammer she'd set aside and took out the last of her heightened emotions on the nails supporting the shelf—not least of which was frustration over his kiss. He knew it would redirect her thoughts to him.

She felt better about her mom, but more confused about her feelings for him than ever. So did she bless him or curse him?

CHAPTER TEN

NOT long after he arrived at work Thursday morning, Trace looked up from where he sat at his desk and saw Nikki approaching the glass doors to the Sheriff's station. She had her purse hooked over her shoulder, her phone to her ear, and maneuvered Mickey's stroller one-handed. Her animated expression told him her attention was wholly focused on the conversation.

He hopped to his feet, expecting the heavy glass door to be an obstacle, but it didn't slow her down at all. She simply turned around and pushed her way in with her nicely rounded backside. He arrived in time to hold the door wide while she swung the stroller around.

"I'm dropping Mickey off now," she said into the phone, making his brow rise in question. "Yes, I called the doctor's service again. They said they spoke to him and he'll meet you at the hospital." To Trace, she mouthed the words, "My sister is in labor."

Yeah, being a former detective, he'd figured that out.

Nikki managed to appear both excited and exasperated as she spoke to her sister.

"Do not call a cab. They'd have to come in from the city, and even coming from El Cajon would take fifteen to twenty minutes. Let me talk to Trace, then I'll be there in five minutes."

She smiled and waved when Lydia came to the counter. "Yes, yes. Amanda, I'm hanging up now. Remember to breathe."

Disconnecting the call, Nikki let out a rush of air, and then she grinned big and did a little dance.

"Amanda is in labor. I'm going to be an aunt."

"I gathered."

"I'm her labor coach. I have to go." She bit her lower lip, the excitement replaced by a conciliatory cringe. "I tried Josh, but he's working. And I didn't know who else—"

"Stop." He held up a hand. "Go. Your sister needs you." And Nikki needed to be with her sister. She'd fret terribly otherwise. "I'll take care of Mickey."

"Thank you for understanding. Here's his diaper bag. I couldn't carry everything, so I left his car seat out by your SUV." She wrinkled her nose sheepishly. "Hopefully nobody is foolish enough to steal from the Sheriff."

"Go. Take care of Amanda." Trace took the diaper bag from her and handed over her purse, which she'd given to him instead. "Do you want me to drive you?"

"No. Wow." Her eyes went soft and wide as she thanked him. "You are so sweet, but we'll be fine. I'll feel better if I have my own car, in case I need to run and get anything. Plus, if my brother-in-law, Dan, doesn't get here, I'll need to drive us home. He's in a training class in Florida. He was supposed to be back on Saturday, but he's going to try to get leave to come home early."

"Hopefully that works out. Call me. Let me know how things are going. Or if you need anything."

"I will." Her phone rang. "Oh, my God, I have to go. I'm going to be an aunt!" She gave him a big hug, Mickey a kiss and then ran out the door.

Trace exchanged glances with Lydia. "So, do you think the roads are safe?" she asked.

"I'd have insisted on driving if I didn't think so. She'll be all right once she's on the road." Slightly bemused, he shook his head. "She thought I was being sweet?"

Lydia shrugged. "Most people don't take their jobs as seriously as you do," she explained.

"It's a serious job."

"Yes, it is. And you do it well. The whole town takes comfort in knowing you take the creed 'To Protect and To Serve' seriously."

He nodded, gratified by the acknowledgment.

"But, Trace, just because your job is serious it doesn't mean you always have to be. The girl thinks you were being sweet. Smile and enjoy the perks."

"Perks, hmm?" Trace had never really thought along those lines. He got paid for his job. Perks were neither necessary nor sought after. But what the hell? He couldn't get much done in his office with Mickey here, and it would save him from having to hunt up a babysitter.

"Daddy." Mickey demanded Trace's attention. He looked down to find little arms in the air. "Up."

He hefted the boy into his arms and then stowed the stroller in his office, out of the way. "Radio me if you need me," he told Lydia on his way out the door. "I'm going to take Mickey for a haircut."

"Oh," she lamented, "he'll lose all those lovely curls."

Trace shoved on his sunglasses. "Exactly."

Ten minutes later he stood in the alien universe of What a Woman Wants, the new beauty salon in town. Arms crossed, he leaned against the wall in clear view of Mickey, who sat on a booster seat at one of the stations.

Mickey shrank back from all the women fawning over him, and Trace plainly read the plea for escape his son sent his way. He commiserated, but held tough.

"Sorry, buddy, but those curls are coming off. You'll thank me when you're older."

"Oh, but they're so adorable," a woman in huge curlers cooed. "How can you think of chopping them off?"

Chirps of agreement rained down on him. He shrugged. "He's a boy. Boys don't have curls. Not in my family."

Oh, man. He sounded just like his dad. Instead of the thought bothering him, Trace decided to cut his dad a little slack. Obviously there were times when a father did know best. "I'm tired of people telling me what a cute daughter I have."

A twitter of giggles told him this crowd just didn't understand.

"Okay, that's enough, ladies. Everyone back to their seats so I have room to work here." Dani Wilder, owner of the shop, shooed the women away. The shapely red-head feathered long fingers through Mickey's fine brown hair. "Mickey, you're being such a good boy."

Her gentle way and soft touch eased Mickey. The exact reason Trace had braved the salon rather than take Mickey to the barbershop for his first haircut.

"So, how short do you want to go?" Dani asked Trace.

"I want him to look like a boy."

"Sheriff, you're obviously a man with some nerve, who knows what he wants," Dani said as she went to work on Mickey's hair. "How do you think the Anderson endowment funds should be used?"

Several female heads cocked in his direction, awaiting his response. Maybe the barbershop would have been a better choice after all.

"Well, Ms. Wilder, it's my job to keep the peace, not add to community unrest, so I think I'll keep my opinion for the voters' box."

She stopped her snipping to send him a chiding glance. "Which means you agree with the men."

"Or he doesn't, but won't allow his opinion to be used in the ongoing argument," said Matilda Sullivan, reigning town matriarch, from her seat two stations down. "The Sheriff is a smart man, keeps a low profile. Snagged himself a pretty sharp gal as a nanny for this young one."

"Mrs. Sullivan," he acknowledged her. Nikki hadn't mentioned meeting the woman, but as a member of the town board Mrs. Sullivan would have been instrumental in approving Nikki to teach at the community center. "Keep your sights off my nanny."

Delighted, the petite woman laughed. "I'm not sure I can promise that. I only met her for a moment, but I've seen her credentials and her references. And my great-grandson says she's *awesome*."

Her exaggerated mimicking of her great-grandson's compliment made their avid audience chuckle.

"Yes, she's quite a catch," he agreed, and immediately cringed internally as he considered how that sounded.

"Well, well, is that a note of personal interest I detect, Sheriff?"

"No," he answered, a little too quickly.

"Now, don't be embarrassed." The matron smiled knowingly. "It's about time you started dating again. It's hard after a loss, but you have to think of your son. You and Ms. Rhodes would make a delightful couple. Personally, I feel a man in a position of civic authority benefits from the input of a spouse." Her chin rose in haughty disdain. "If our current mayor had a wife and family he might better understand the need for a cultural influence in our town."

Trace ducked his chin to keep from displaying his amusement. "Mrs. Sullivan, our current mayor is your grandson."

She actually sniffed. "Yes, and if Cord had listened to me and settled down to domestic bliss years ago, he'd be better qualified to address the needs of all the citizens of Paradise Pines."

"Ladies, you're making this into a bigger issue than it needs—" He cut off when eight heads in various stages of coiffure snapped his way. Man, the comment about him and Nikki making a good couple must have thrown him off more than he thought, or he would have guarded his words better.

"*We're* making this a bigger issue than necessary?"

Head at a regal tilt, ice dripped from the matriarch's words.

Uh-oh, he'd riled the beast.

"I just meant—"

"You were quite clear. But we're not the ones who already had plans drawn up for a sports complex *before* the announcement of the endowment."

"Yeah," chorused through the room.

"On second thought, Sheriff, I'm glad to hear there's nothing personal between you and Nikki Rhodes. She and my grandson would make a lovely couple. And she may be just what he needs to sway him. A sweet young thing with a master's in Child Development might be just the weapon we need."

And the beast had a vicious bite.

"All done," Dani said, her pronouncement a cheerful trill in the tense room.

Rescued. Before the atmosphere got any more hostile, he grabbed Mickey and made good his escape, wondering all the while if a lovely couple trumped a delightful couple.

* * *

Nikki leaned against the wall and stared into the nursery at the beautiful sight of her new nephew. Little Anthony Amare had given his mother a bit of a bad time. But you'd never know it by the peacefulness of his slumber.

Exhausted, emotion overflowing within her, Nikki needed the wall to hold her up. The day had been long, fraught with moments of drama between extended periods of waiting. Amanda had gone through twelve hours of labor, only to be rushed into surgery for an emergency C-Section at the last moment.

It tore at Nikki's heart that she hadn't been able to go into surgery with her sister, but when the decision came they'd had to move too fast for Nikki to suit up.

The baby hadn't been dropping down as he should, and it turned out the cord had been wrapped around his neck. The thought of what could have happened made her heart pound double time.

She was thankful, so thankful, that both baby and Mom had come through okay her knees threatened to buckle from relief. And the arrival of Dan added to the joy of the event.

Knowing mom, dad and baby would soon be together brought tears to Nikki's eyes. Amanda had been in post-op until a few minutes ago. Of course Nikki had sent Dan into her. And here she waited, keeping watch over Anthony until they came for him, too. The family deserved their privacy, but after the long, emotional day, it left her feeling a little alone.

She couldn't help but think of Trace, standing alone

in front of a nursery window fourteen months ago, shocked by his wife's death and bewildered and overwhelmed by the birth of his son. How did you celebrate the one while mourning the other?

What a nightmare for a man who claimed he didn't do emotion well.

No wonder he'd accepted his in-laws' offer of help. How easy it must have been to let distance grow between him and Mickey. And what a shame when they both needed each other so much.

At least they were finally finding each other.

Inside the nursery, little Anthony scowled and a lump rose in Nikki's throat. Oh, yeah, he was a little Rhodes; he looked just like her dad when he frowned.

She traced his cheek on the glass window, a new wave of emotion making her hand shake. How she wished her parents were here to see their first grandchild.

"You'd be so proud," she whispered. "I never knew, Mom, how big love for a baby could be. Not until Mickey. And now Anthony. I knew love, yeah. You and dad gave us that always. It was a constant in our lives. But this is so huge, so wonderful and scary. I know you're up there, watching over us. And that Trace is right, and you probably don't even remember our last fight. But I do, and I'm sorry."

"Nikki?" A hand cupped the small of her back as a man stopped next to her. "Are you okay?"

Startled, she half turned—and looked into Trace's calm green eyes. Without thought she threw herself into his arms, and sighed as he pulled her close into his warmth.

"I'm so glad you're here," she said into his chest. It only made it more perfect that Mickey slept, crushed between them. Her two guys in her arms. Nothing could be better.

"Hey." Trace lifted her chin on a gentle knuckle. "*Are* you okay?"

"I'm fine. I'm wonderful." She ran a hand over Mickey's new haircut. "Big change."

"It had to be done."

"Looks good." She pointed out Anthony in the nursery, and grinned as he admired the baby. "Mom and baby are both healthy and beautiful. Dan got here twenty minutes ago. Life is good."

"Then why the tears?" His concern, the sincere caring in his gaze, wiped her loneliness out in a single blow.

"No tears." She denied the wetness on her cheeks. "Not today." And, using all her courage, launched herself onto her toes, wrapped her arms around his neck and pulled him into a kiss.

"Nikki," he groaned. Immediately he shifted her into the shelter of his free shoulder, deepened the angle of the kiss and devoured her mouth with his.

As an energizer, passion really packed a kick. Nikki gave as good as she got, tangling tongues, drinking in the taste of him, immersing herself in the embrace. He felt so good she longed to find a flat surface and take the sizzling sensations to the next level.

Finally time and place sank in, and she fell back on her heels, but she didn't break away from him. Instead she snuggled close. The baby was born, Dan was back, finally she could relax her guard.

His hand, warm and soothing, curled into her hair, making her feel cherished.

"What was that for?" Desire deepened his pitch to velvet-covered gravel, rough and sensual.

She licked her lips, tempted to tell him how happy she was to see him, how much she loved that he'd made such an effort to come see her. But it would be a selfish announcement, and it would probably scare the bejeezus out of him. So she simply shrugged and said, "It's a day for miracles."

He raised his brows, but didn't pursue it. Instead, he laid his lips softly on hers again, drawing out the moment before lifting his head. "Congratulations, Aunt Nikki."

Tears clogged her throat. Closing her eyes, she rested against him, savoring the warmth and contentment of being held by the man she loved, stealing these precious moments against a lifetime without him. Now that he and Mickey were bonding, she'd sent out résumés both to schools in San Diego and to a couple of the bordering counties.

"Not that I'm complaining, but why are you here?" she asked him.

"I got your message that you'd be staying over, and I brought you a comfort package."

"Really?" She leaned her head back to look up at him. His cheeks were a ruddy red—but from lingering arousal or embarrassment? Perhaps a bit of both? "You're so sweet."

"You keep saying that, but I'm not sweet at all. I'm practical."

"Uh-huh. It's practical to bring a baby out at eleven o'clock at night to bring me a comfort package?"

The red deepened in his cheeks. "It was only nine when I picked up your message."

"Don't fight it. You're sweet."

"I'd much rather be practical. Or tough. Even cute is better than sweet."

"Well, you are all of those things," she allowed, to make him happy, but she couldn't lie. "And you're sweet, too."

She laughed at his disgruntled grimace. Patting down his pockets, she demanded, "What did you bring me?"

"Hold on." He set her back on her own weight. "It's in a bag here somewhere."

"A bag?" She stepped back to look, and nearly put her foot through the pretty pink package. It stood as high as her knees, and the width spanned a good eight inches. No tissue paper, and the handles were tied together—clear signs he'd done the packaging himself, which only made the gesture more special. A smaller blue bag had toppled on its side. "Oh, my. Trace, what did you get?"

"It's not much. I figured you'd have brought the essentials. These are just a few things to make a long night more comfortable. The smaller gift is for Amanda."

"I love surprise presents." All signs of weariness disappeared as she peeked inside and spied something pale blue and fuzzy. "Let's find somewhere comfortable to sit down. I can't wait to open it."

As she led the way to the lobby, she told him about the delivery, and Dan's late arrival.

"So actually, now Dan's here, I may grab a ride home. I'll check with Amanda, but I'm sure they'd prefer to be alone."

"You can always come back tomorrow," he assured her. "You don't need to worry about Mickey. I've arranged for a sitter."

"You don't mind if I take another day?" In the lobby she sank unto a sofa and patted the spot beside her. Trace laid Mickey down, then sat beside her.

He shrugged her concern away. "You've covered for me plenty. Besides, it's not every day a nanny becomes an aunt."

"No." His easy acceptance of the altered schedule surprised her. This was not the same rigid man she'd met a month and a half ago. Mickey had been as good for his dad as Trace had been for Mickey.

"What did you get me?" She dug into the bag and found a plush fleece blanket, slipper socks and a travel pillow, all in shades of baby blue. "Trace, this is too much. I feel bad, now, that I'm not staying."

"Don't be ridiculous. You always go out of your way to see to our comfort. I wanted to do it. It's not like you can't use these things at home. And, yes, it's okay to lend anything you want to Dan. My feelings won't be hurt."

"Well, thank you." She didn't let the fact the gift

came from a sense of obligation upset her. Much. The point was he'd made the effort. "Am I so easy to read?"

"Hardly." An incredulous laugh escaped him. "You constantly keep me guessing. But in some things, like the comfort of those you care about, you are very predictable."

"Uh-huh?" Somewhat appeased, she loaded the items back into the bag. "Oh, here's Dan."

Nikki introduced Trace to her brother-in-law, and then Dan caught them up on Amanda's condition. "They moved her back to her room and brought the baby in, so she's pretty jazzed right now. She wants to see you. You should come, too," he said to Trace.

"Yes," Nikki urged him, "you have to give Amanda your gift. Oh." Disappointment bit sharp when he shifted Mickey in his arms to pick up the blue bag. Hospital rules didn't allow children in the maternity rooms. "I don't think they'll let us bring Mickey."

Trace lifted a dark brow. "I have a badge. There won't be any problem."

CHAPTER ELEVEN

"DIDN'T Amanda look radiant with her son in her arms?" Nikki mused once they were in the SUV on the way home, at a little after one in the morning.

Trace merged onto the freeway, headed east. Amanda had looked unkempt, uncomfortable and exhausted. Exactly as you'd expect after twelve hours of labor and surgery. And, yes, she'd lit up the room with her joy and contentment.

"A mother and her babe are a beautiful thing," Trace agreed.

"You were wonderful tonight." Nikki laid a warm hand on his knee. The heat of her touch blazed straight to his lap. The traffic was light this hour of the morning, so he chanced a glance at her, and then did a double-take.

Her eyes were luminous, shining bright with…love?

For a moment the earth rolled on its axis and his world exploded, becoming bright and perfect. And *right*. As if he'd finally found his life's path. And Nikki walked it with him.

No, he had to be mistaken. Nikki didn't love him. She loved her family. That was it: the love lighting her eyes was for the family she'd just left behind. That explained it.

Which was a relief, right? So why did he suddenly feel deprived and lost?

"Your gift for Amanda was perfect. How did you know to bring her snacks?"

"I did my homework when Donna was expecting. The mother isn't allowed to eat or doesn't feel like eating during labor. After the baby is born she's ready for something to snack on. And I threw in the slipper socks because it can get cold in the hospital."

"Oh, Trace," Nikki breathed. She turned toward him in her seat. "How thoughtful you've been, when this visit must have been very traumatic for you. The memories it must have brought back... Are you okay?"

"I told you I was no good at emotion. My marriage was a perfect example of that. We were compatible; she wanted to get married. I agreed. It was that simple— until it got complicated. She began to complain about my hours. Then she wanted to quit work and have a baby. At first I resisted, but she got pregnant anyway."

"You must have felt trapped. Your sense of honor and duty would have required you to stay with them."

He sat in silence for a moment, remembering his frustration and hurt at having his feelings in such a big decision ignored. It occurred to him that Nikki knew him better after only a month or two of working together than Donna had over three years of marriage.

"At first I was angry. But you're right. Duty and obligation kicked in. I'd vowed for better or worse, and I determined a baby would make things better. Donna wouldn't be so lonely. She'd have her child."

"How did Donna feel about the compromise?"

"We were making the best of it. Donna was excited about the baby, and I was glad to see her happy and occupied."

"You would have made it work," she said, her faith in him obvious, but her tone held an odd edge he couldn't identify.

"I like to think so." He would have tried, *had* tried, but he wondered now if mediocre feelings would have been enough to hold them together through the long haul.

"When she died and Mickey lived it seemed like one big cosmic joke. Kill off the one who wanted the baby and leave him with a messed up dude who knows nothing about childcare and less about providing for someone else's emotional well-being. I was so relieved when Donna's parents said they'd take him. For Mickey's sake more than my own. But it turns out I still messed up."

"You did what was right for everyone concerned at the time. Plus you changed your whole life, your job, your residence, your lifestyle, to make a home for Mickey."

"But I left him with his grandparents longer than I needed to."

"Mostly out of compassion for your mother-in-law."

"But not all. I was no better prepared for a one-year-old than a newborn."

"Yeah, well, a lot of child rearing is on-the-job training."

"You're too soft on me."

"You're too hard on yourself."

He squeezed her hand. "Mickey and I are lucky to have you. You're going to make a wonderful aunt."

Twenty minutes later Trace pulled into his driveway, placed the SUV in Park, and with a tired sigh shut off the engine. He glanced to the right. Nikki sat slumped against the door, a hand curled under her cheek, sound asleep.

He hated to wake her after such a long, emotional day, but she'd be more comfortable in her own bed. Cupping her shoulder, he shook her gently. Nothing. He shook a little harder. She shifted and resettled against the door, clearly out of it.

He decided to take Mickey in first and come back for Nikki. He lifted his son against his shoulder. Such a slight weight. Trace barely remembered him as a newborn. Born early, he'd had to stay in the hospital for a week while his lungs and weight stabilized. Fighting through the shock and grief of losing Donna, Trace had spent days planning a funeral and nights sitting next to an incubator.

It had been the worst time of his life.

He'd been so grateful for his in-laws' offer to take Mickey. Now, as he settled his son in his bed, Trace was thankful to finally have his son in his custody, and he prayed for the strength and fortitude to be a good parent. With Nikki's help, he just might have a chance.

He returned to the SUV for her. Carefully opening

her door, he cupped her shoulder to keep her from falling and accepted her weight as she slumped sideways. She mumbled, but didn't awaken.

"Nikki, wake up now," he urged her. "We're home."

"Home," she said, and laid her head on his shoulder.

"Come on, sweetheart, wake up."

"Hmm…" She sighed, and nestled closer.

"Okay, then." He swung her up into his arms, hooked her purse over his elbow, shoved the door shut with his hip and headed inside.

As he climbed the steps to the front deck she roused. "I can walk," she murmured, even as she circled his neck and snuggled against him.

"I've got you," he whispered into her hair. How he longed to carry her straight through to his bed, where he could hold her close during the night and wake up with her in the morning.

He knew in that moment she'd reached depths in him he'd never allowed anyone to touch. Not even with Donna had he ever looked beyond the moment. With Nikki he saw them sitting on the back deck, hands linked, as they watched grandchildren playing in the yard.

He shuddered, recognizing things had gone too far, knowing she deserved better than a ready-made family complete with two dysfunctional males. But wanting, oh, wanting so badly to reach out and grasp love, to know the true meaning of family and commitment.

Inside, he set her on the couch while he went to hunt up the key to her apartment. When he came back, he found her sprawled full-length on the couch.

"Nikki," he called softly, lifting her torso up and sliding into the spot next to her so she couldn't lie back down. "It's time to go to bed."

She opened sleepy amber eyes, blinked at him and smiled.

"Stay here," she said, and then she climbed into his arms, pushing him into the corner in the process, and sprawled next to him. "Home."

She was asleep again before he could protest. Not that he wanted to object. Hugging her close, he shifted his legs up onto the couch to tangle with hers.

Yes, again the world felt right.

He sighed and let his body relax. Surrounded by the sweet scent of apple blossom and woman, savoring the lush feel of Nikki in his arms, he drifted off to sleep.

"Stupid cell service." Nikki clicked the "end" button on her cell phone and tossed it in the passenger seat. The law restricted her from using the phone while driving, but since she hadn't moved more than a quarter mile in twenty-five minutes she figured she was safe. Unfortunately, she had no service, so it didn't matter anyway.

Cars stretched out on the freeway as far as she could see in both directions. Glancing in the rearview mirror, she checked on Mickey. He sat happily in his car seat, eating a teething biscuit.

"I don't know how you can be so calm. Your daddy is going to have my hide if he gets home before we do." She tapped her fingers on the steering wheel. She should have been home thirty minutes ago. "The radio says there's an accident involving a semi near Lake Jennings Road."

The on and off ramps had both been closed, and they were talking about an oil spill. She'd just passed Los Coches, which meant there was no off ramp between her and the accident. Until the road cleared, nobody was going anywhere.

"Daddy?" Mickey called out, and clapped his hands.

"Yeah." Nikki grinned at his response. "He's your favorite person, huh? I'm so happy you two have become good buds."

Trace hadn't been pleased with her decision to drive Amanda into town. With a high wind advisory in effect, and thunderstorms threatening, he'd considered the trip frivolous and unnecessary. Of course that had only made her more determined to go.

Hold back because of the weather? In San Diego County, with its generally mild climate and where the weather forecasters were wrong as often as they were right? Uh-uh.

Rain started to splatter the windshield.

"Oh, wonderful. That's the icing on the cake." Could it get any worse?

"Cake?" Mickey repeated, recognizing one of his favorite treats.

"Sorry, buddy, no cake."

Mickey threw the teething biscuit and demanded, "Cake! Cake! Cake!"

"Mickey, stop."

Now she'd done it. Overdue for his afternoon nap, the usually even-tempered baby went into a cranky fit.

The bland biscuit—she didn't blame Mickey for preferring cake—had been the last of her distractions. Rather than scold him for his behavior, she talked gently to him, giving him her full attention. She explained where they were, and what was happening and promised she'd get him home as soon as she could. He didn't understand the words, but he responded to her reassuring tone and attentive manner and soon settled down. It also helped when she dug Boo out of the diaper bag.

If only Daddy would be so easy to calm down.

All right, so her contrariness had gotten the better of her. But it wasn't all her fault. She treasured her independence, and Trace's suggestions often sounded more like orders. Plus, she'd already promised Amanda a ride into town to meet Dan. It was her sister's first outing since having the baby, and she'd so been looking forward to it. Nikki hadn't had the heart to disappoint her.

But she despised hurting Trace.

She checked her cell again. Nothing. She always lost service through these hills.

In a few minutes he'd be home. He wouldn't know where they were. He'd worry—especially with the weather turning bad.

Hopefully he'd hear about the accident and realize she was stuck.

She'd found such sweet slumber in his arms the other night. How she wished it had turned into more. But, no, he'd let her sleep while he got Mickey up, dressed and fed. Only when Trace was ready to walk out the door had he woken her.

Sleeping in his arms, she had felt cherished and above all else safe. No need to play big sister, nanny, teacher, housekeeper. Not during the hours he guarded her sleep. He'd gone to a lot of trouble, risked some pretty heavy memories for her benefit.

Surely that meant he cared for her beyond what she provided for his son?

A wicked grin formed as she remembered the lingering sizzle in the air ever since. Oh, yeah, he cared. Then she sobered, hoping this stunt—and the anxiety it would bring—didn't ruin everything.

"Trace, call on line three." Lydia's voice floated down the hall, a sure sign she and the new phone system weren't on speaking terms yet.

He picked up the line. "Sheriff Oliver."

"Mr. Oliver?" a brisk voice greeted him. "I'm with the Irvine Central School District. I need to verify employment for Ms. Nikki Rhodes, can you help me?"

Trace dropped his pen on the desk and sat back in his chair, giving his entire attention to the phone call.

"Yes, Ms. Rhodes works for me. What is this in regard to?"

"I'm sorry, I'm not at liberty to say—"

He cut off the privacy mumbo-jumbo. "But you're with the Irvine Central School District? That must mean she's applied for a position there."

"I'm not allowed to discuss the applicant's business."

She confirmed his suspicion with her officious disclaimer. "Would you be willing to answer a few questions? How long has Ms. Rhodes been working for you?"

Trace answered the questions on autopilot, while his mind wheeled with the possibility of losing Nikki. Why hadn't she told him she was applying for a job? Was it something he'd done? Something he hadn't done?

Like holding her in his arms all night long and not making sweet love to her. The hardest thing he'd ever done was to leave her sleeping alone the next morning.

And now she would be leaving. A fist twisted in his gut, a cold sense of dread enveloping him.

Of course he knew she'd always intended going back to teaching, but surely she would tell him if she had applied for a position.

Obviously not. And that hurt.

"The résumé indicates she also lives with you. Is that correct?"

"She has an apartment on my property, yes."

"Thank you, sir. Just one last question. Would you consider rehiring Ms. Rhodes in the future?"

Rehire her? Forget that. He didn't want her to go.

Trace drove up to the house as the first raindrops fell, not surprised to see Nikki's car missing from the curb. Numerous unanswered calls to the house since his conversation with the Irvine Central School District had already told him she wasn't home.

A slow-burning anger brewed. She'd gone against his wishes and driven Amanda into town to meet her husband and now she'd got stuck behind the accident blocking Freeway Eight.

Hell, he prayed that was all that had delayed Nikki. If she wanted to risk her neck, he couldn't stop her. But she'd had no right to take Mickey with her.

He tried her cell again, and again it went straight to voice mail.

Lightning lashed the sky as he entered the cool, prematurely darkened house. No lights burned, and there was no sense of the warm welcome he'd become accustomed to since Nikki came to stay.

But she hadn't come to stay; she'd come to work. And now she meant to leave him, to work somewhere else. Thunder boomed, and the rip of lightning outside mimicked what he felt inside: torn apart with anger, loss and pain.

He paced, needing an outlet for his rage.

Where was she? Where was his son?

For so long he'd fought the reality of being a parent, believing any child of his was better off with any family besides him. Yet every day he spent with Mickey made Trace realize how wrong he'd been.

Mickey was a miracle. For better or worse, he loved Trace. And his unconditional trust and affection touched Trace beyond anything he'd ever known.

Trace prayed nothing would happen to Mickey when he'd just found him. God, he loved his son.

Seeking action, Trace called the station, asked Lydia to check on the traffic board and give him current road conditions and accident reports. A few small collisions had popped up—no fatalities, thank the Lord—and they'd cleared a couple of lanes near the semi rollover on eight. Traffic had begun moving through the area.

Relieved to know there'd been no accident-related deaths, he hung up and went to check the window again. Five minutes later Nikki pulled up in front of the house.

He cleared the door and took the steps two at a time to reach her car. She was already out, struggling to release Mickey from his car seat.

"Let me." He moved her aside to reach the sleeping boy. "Where the hell have you been?" he demanded. Not waiting for an answer, he snapped, "Next time you want to kidnap my son, leave your cell phone on."

"I know you're angry." She brushed rain off her cheeks. "But I promise you I exhausted every avenue before taking Mickey with me."

"I'm sure you tried real hard." He grabbed a blanket from the diaper bag, tucked it around Mickey and then thrust the bag in her hands before heading inside.

"I did try." She followed hard on his heels. "I had Josh lined up, but he got called into work. I only know of three other people you'd allow to watch him. I couldn't reach one and the other two were busy."

"Then you shouldn't have gone." He left her to close the front door, intent on getting Mickey to his bed.

"You say that, but you weren't here." Nikki stopped in the bedroom doorway, heartfelt in her efforts to convince him she was right and he was wrong.

Mickey stirred as Trace changed him. He grinned at

Trace, mentioned something about cake, and went back to sleep when Trace settled him in his crib.

"Amanda was so excited about this outing." Nikki continued her explanation. "She was in tears when I suggested not going. Her doctor has told her not to drive for a while, but I knew she would drive herself if I didn't take her. I determined that was the bigger danger."

"Leave your sister out of this. You didn't want to hear a word I said after I mentioned the weather."

"That's because this is San Diego. They're always wrong about the weather."

As if cued, a loud boom echoed overhead, followed by lightning strobing across the sky, backlighting the windows and illuminating Nikki's features in stark relief. He looked for remorse, found none.

With nature on his side, he didn't have to say a word; he simply arched a dark eyebrow.

She propped her hands on her hips. "Anyway, the weather's not why I was late. There was—"

"A rollover accident, blocking the freeway. I know."

Her shoulders slumped in relief. "So you did hear about that? *Good.*"

"Good? How is any of this good?"

"You figured out where I was. I kept trying to call you, but the service was out on my cell."

"I didn't know where you were! I speculated, hoped, prayed, but for all I knew my son could have been under that semi."

Her defiance drained away, along with the color from her face. "That's a terrible thing to say."

"It was a terrible thing to visualize."

"Oh, Trace." She took a tentative step toward him. "You have to know I love Mickey. I'd die before I let anything happen to him."

His anger faded at her words. Any pretense that his overwhelming concern had been for Mickey alone disappeared as he recognized his rage for what it truly was: a poor disguise for the fear he felt at the possibility of losing the people he'd come to love, of losing her.

He bridged the space between them and framed her face in his hands.

"That is not an acceptable alternative," he told her, before claiming her mouth with urgent need.

CHAPTER TWELVE

THE demand of Trace's mouth took over Nikki's senses. Defenses well and truly down, she returned his kisses with eager demands of her own. His arms tightened around her as he lifted and carried her across the hall. She wrapped her arms around him and clung. Sweet relief added the tang of tears to the embrace.

He was right. Nikki hated to be told what to do, and she'd thought she knew better. But she'd been wrong and she knew it.

The thought of Trace waiting here, worried about his son being crushed in a car accident—just like his wife had been—made Nikki sick to her stomach. It had always been about more than the weather, and she should have honored Trace's wishes.

"Hey, no crying." He pulled back to kiss the wetness from the corner of her eyes, to trace the path of despair and erase it with tenderness. He lowered her to the bed, his weight causing the bed to dip as he joined her.

His pace slowed, relaxed, but was no less demanding. Gentle strokes and featherlight touches stoked the flames of desire started by fierce caresses. He delayed only long enough to ask about protection before taking the loving up a notch.

The whistle of the wind and the staccato beat of rain against glass, accompanied by the booming drum of thunder, lent music to the tempest brewing inside the sultry heat of the bedroom. Lightning cracked as they arched in perfect harmony, punctuating Nikki's cry of ecstasy.

Nikki buttered toast, humming a jazzy little tune under her breath. It was a beautiful day. Mickey sat at the table, eating dry fruity loops, waiting for Trace to finish his shower.

Nothing was different from every other morning of the past two months—except everything was different.

"Someone is in a good mood this morning," Trace said as he stepped around her to grab a plate from the counter. "Hey, buddy." He rubbed his hand affectionately over Mickey's head on his way to his customary seat at the table.

Though his tone was more subdued than teasing, she responded with a sassy grin.

"I won't deny it. I'm in a fabulous mood." Picking up two dishes, she carried them to the table, placing a plate of toast in the middle of the table and a bowl of scrambled eggs on Mickey's tray.

She hesitated beside Trace, to see if she'd get a good-morning kiss, but he dug into his food, not looking up.

"I'd think *you'd* be in a better mood," she said, on her way back to the kitchen for her own plate.

His green gaze shot up to meet hers. As enigmatic as always. She failed to read his mood, but got a clue when he asked, "No regrets?"

"I regret making you worry." She slid into the seat to his right. "But spending the night with you? No. What about you?" She tore off a piece of toast, took a tiny bite. "It did get a little out of control last night." She cleared her throat. "Twice."

The thunderstorm had caused some flooding, and he'd been called away not long after they first made love. She'd fallen asleep on the couch, waiting for him to get home, and woken up when he'd picked her up and carried her back to his bed for another round of luscious loving.

"Exactly. I didn't give you a lot of choice."

"Oh, Trace." Nikki reached for his hand. "Is that what's bothering you? Believe me, I was exactly where I wanted to be."

"You're sure?"

"Absolutely. I've wanted to be with you ever since you kissed me at the station."

He glanced at Mickey, as if gauging his reaction.

She sent him a wry grin. "I don't think you need to worry. He's a mite young to understand." She looked down at her plate and the shredded pieces of toast. "It sounds like you're the one with regrets."

"No, of course not." He set his fork down. "Last night was amazing. You were incredible." His hand turned under hers, his fingers lacing with hers. "I've wanted to be with you, too."

"Really?" Pleased, she flushed.

"Oh, yeah." He lifted her hand to his mouth and kissed her knuckles. "You've taught me there are times when control is highly overrated." Then he released her and stood. "But I have to go."

"Oh. Of course." Flustered by the news he'd been lusting after her, she watched as he took his plate to the counter, then returned to kiss Mickey's head.

"Bye-bye, Daddy!" Mickey called.

Trace rounded the table and stopped next to her chair. He lifted her chin and planted a hard, passionate kiss on her lips. "See you later."

It was a promise that had heat flooding her cheeks while she watched him make his exit. After he was gone, she continued to sit in stunned confusion. From his stilted responses she really had begun to believe he regretted what had happened between them. She understood why, of course.

Honor and duty meant everything to Trace. For him to take advantage of someone in his care and under his protection would be repugnant to him. She liked to think their relationship had progressed beyond employer-employee to friendship long ago, and this was just the next step. But she accepted Trace would be more sensitive to the situation.

Still, the notion he felt shame for what had been one of the most beautiful nights of her life nearly broke her heart.

She hoped she'd settled any concerns he had.

If his parting kiss meant anything, then she had to believe he'd accepted they were both consenting adults, capable of handling an intimate relationship.

Of course that begged the question: could she handle a relationship with him?

She loved Trace. And Mickey. A glance at the boy showed he'd managed to get as much egg on his tray and himself as he had in his mouth. Rising, she made quick work of cleaning him up, before placing him in his playpen with a few of his favorite toys.

"Have fun, kiddo." Even as she kissed his head and left him to play, her mind roiled with emotions.

She returned to the kitchen to clean up. So much of the time they'd spent together had been right here, in the dining room and kitchen. Had that given her a false sense of family? Of kinship with father and son? Had proximity caused her to manufacture feelings—?

No, that didn't feel right. She loved Trace. He made her feel alive, yet safe. His courage and honor. His seriousness and the fact he believed in what he did. The way he kept saying he was no good at emotions, yet he was infinitely gentle with Mickey and had honestly grown to love his son.

In truth, they worked well together. Their ideas of child-rearing and household scheduling jived so well she rarely felt suffocated by his need for control— though she'd come to realize that was more her view of him than a reality. His was more a natural confidence, paired with discipline and decisiveness. He didn't have to have his way; when she gave input he listened. He was considerate, always letting her know when he'd be late, and intelligent, and he needed her to make him laugh.

Oh, yeah, she loved him.

And after last night she believed he cared about her, too. But was it enough to make a future together?

"So, are you going to take the job?" Amanda asked, from where she sat feeding Anthony in her small living room.

Nikki put the finishing touches to broccoli salad for their lunch. She'd finally listened to yesterday's cell messages on her way to her sister's, and one had been from Irvine Central School District. When she'd returned the call, they'd offered her a teaching position.

"I don't know," she equivocated, drizzling her special poppyseed dressing over both salads. She set the bowl of dressing on the counter and licked her finger, enjoying the tangy sweetness. One of her mother's recipes. "It's middle school kids."

Amanda took the plate Nikki handed her, then opened her arms so Nikki could take the sleeping baby and place him in his cradle next to the rocker.

"So?" Amanda demanded. "I know you prefer the little guys, but middle school kids need good teachers, too."

"Of course." Nikki waved away the obviousness of that comment. "But—"

She stopped, unable to come up with anything that wasn't a flat-out excuse for the truth. Which was she didn't want to go.

"But?" Amanda prompted.

Nikki just shook her head.

"Oh, Nikki." Amanda rocked forward in the chair to rest a hand on Nikki's arm. "You're not worried about leaving me, are you? Because Irvine is only a few hours away. We'd see each other all the time."

"Not like we do now," Nikki protested. This was one of her main objections. "I'd miss all the important milestones, all Anthony's firsts."

"You love to teach. And you'll be able to afford the condo you've been wanting. I can't believe you're not jumping on this opportunity."

"You don't understand."

"Then make me understand. Do you have another plan? You've always known what you want for your future. This isn't like you."

Nikki set her salad on the coffee table. "It's not my future I'm worried about right now. It's my life."

Amanda narrowed her eyes and scrutinized Nikki. She groaned. "Oh, no."

"I'm in love with Trace," Nikki confessed, reaching for her iced tea to avoid meeting her sister's eyes.

"Nikki, Nikki," Amanda commiserated, and then her eyes went wide. "Oh, my goodness, you *slept* with Trace. I knew it," she crowed, waking Anthony so he cried. "It's okay, baby," Amanda cooed, setting her salad bowl aside to pick up her son. "All is good. Auntie Nikki just got her some last night."

"Amanda!" Nikki said, outraged, looking to where Mickey played on a blanket on the floor. "There are babies present."

"Yeah, right. Mickey is going to run home and tell Daddy we were talking about him. Come on," Amanda coaxed her. "Give up the details. That man is hot."

Nikki fanned herself, agreeing without words, and actually needing the cooling air as memories of the night flashed through her head. Reliving Trace's slow, sure touch, his demanding kisses and driving passion, spiked her temperature despite the air-conditioner blowing full blast.

"That's one word to describe him."

When she left it at that, Amanda pleaded for more. "You can't leave me hanging."

"Let's just say the man is thorough in everything he does."

"So it was wonderful?"

"Oh, yeah."

"I'm so happy for you." Amanda did a little dance with Anthony. "All kidding aside, he's been good for you. I'm so glad you found your way to each other."

"What do you mean, he's been good for me?" Nikki asked, surprised by the comment.

"I've noticed the difference in you these past couple of months. You're more serene, less worried about details and protecting your freedom."

"Really? Huh." Now Amanda mentioned it, Nikki realized she *did* feel more relaxed these days, less pressured to exert her independence—not counting her arrogant episode yesterday. Another indication Trace was the right guy for her.

"Has he asked you to stay?"

"I haven't told him about the offer."

"Nikki!"

"What? I just picked up the message on the way over here."

"So, do you think he'll ask you?"

There was the question of the day.

Before she could answer, her cell rang. Perfect timing. She scrambled for her purse and pulled out her phone. Five minutes later she hung up.

"That didn't sound good," Amanda said.

"No." Nikki swallowed around the lump in her throat. "That was the nanny agency. Trace contacted them today to ask for a new nanny."

Nikki hit the bungalow at full steam. She was surprised to see Trace's official vehicle in the drive. Lucky for him she hadn't had to hunt him down to deliver Mickey into his care, because she had a few words to say to the sniveling coward he probably wouldn't want the world to hear.

The rat hadn't even had the guts to tell her to leave to her face.

Hmm. She tapped her fingers on the steering wheel; maybe she should wait until he left? Then she could pack in peace and find him some place highly public to have her showdown. Why should she care what people thought of him when he didn't care what her agency thought of her?

He deserved it.

But Mickey didn't. She checked on him in the rear-view mirror. He'd fallen asleep on the ride from

Amanda's. He'd come so far. Going from a sad little boy, emotionally and physically, to a healthy toddler all giggles and hugs.

She was going to miss him so much.

Better to make the break as fast and as quietly as possible for his sake. With that in mind, she let herself inside.

Trace was in the kitchen, sandwich makings in front of him. Ignoring him, she carried Mickey to his bedroom and put him in his crib. Heart breaking, she ran her hand through his big-boy hair. "I love you, baby," she whispered. "Have a happy life."

When she turned, Trace stood in the doorway. "Hey, I came home hoping we could have lunch."

"Right. Even the condemned get a last meal." She brushed past him.

"What? Hey." He grabbed her hand and drew her to a stop. "You're upset."

"You think?" She twisted her wrist to free her hand. "Let go. You don't get to touch me anymore."

He frowned, but released her. "What is wrong with you?"

She shook her head and walked away. Fast and quiet, she reminded herself. For Mickey.

"Nikki?" For a weak-kneed slug he easily kept pace with her, staying hard on her heels. "Would you stop and talk to me?"

"Now you want to talk? Oh, I forgot. You're real good at talking. To everyone but me."

"Okay—enough." No longer conciliatory, he blocked

her way when she headed for the back door leading to her apartment. "You're not going anywhere. Calm down and tell me what changed between this morning and this afternoon."

His supposed obtuseness chafed, making her angrier. "Don't pretend you don't know. You may be a coward, but at least own up to what you did."

"Coward?" he said, low and fierce. "Explain."

She walked away, put the couch between them. She needed distance. More, she needed to pack and get away from here—before she lost any more of herself.

She paced to the fireplace and back. She couldn't do it. She couldn't walk away without some answers.

"You tell me. I was beginning to believe you were going to make the change from broken, unemotional man to a loving man and father. I was wrong."

"I'm not broken," he denied, crossing his arms over his chest, closing himself off. "And I warned you I was no good at emotion."

"Oh, did that sting?" It was wrong to take pleasure in hurting him, but something—rage, or a dim hope she might break through the stone fortress he called a heart so Mickey didn't suffer the same fate in the future—kept her pushing. "The truth usually does. And when you're so absorbed with dodging the pain of loss and rejection you can't see the good for the bad, then, yeah, you're broken."

"You don't know what you're talking about."

"I know I've heard the bad parts of your past—how your mom abandoned you and your father, how he was an unemotional man. But I've never heard any good memories."

His eyelids flickered, but nothing else moved on his frozen features.

"Before your mother left were there any happy moments? Laughter? Hugs? If not, you were better off without her. And she shouldn't be given any power over your future at all."

"She has no power over me."

"Oh, she does. You're afraid to trust your feelings because you're afraid it won't be enough, like it wasn't enough for her, and you'll be left hurting again. She has power over you, over Mickey, even over me. And it infuriates me."

"You're leaving. Just like she did."

"No, you're pushing me away. I won't stay where I'm not wanted. Life is too short. I'll find someone who will love me back and I'll be happy." Continuing to pace, she wrapped both arms around herself, trying to hold in the pain. "That's one lesson I learned from my mother. I was so worried about finding and protecting my own personal freedom I stayed away from her, for fear she'd steal some of it away from me. Instead I lost precious time with her I'll never get back."

"Nikki." He came around the couch, but she held up a hand to ward him off. He stopped. "How did I push you away? I'm here. I came home for lunch in the middle of the day to see you."

"Please." She didn't bother to keep the disdain from her voice. "If you wanted me to leave why didn't you just talk to me, instead of calling my agency and putting my professional reputation at risk?"

"I didn't…" He hesitated.

Nikki hugged herself, waiting for his explanation, for the big reveal.

The silence ended with Mickey's cries.

She closed her eyes. That was it, then. She'd never know what had driven Trace to push her away. Oh, who was she kidding? She'd just laid out all the reasons.

"You'd better get Mickey," she told Trace. "I need to pack." Walking around him, she let herself out of the house.

Trace watched Nikki walk out of his life. A racking sadness overwhelmed him, rooting him to the spot. His chest felt hollow where his heart should be.

Almost immediately the door opened and she reappeared. Hope soared.

"I can't do this now. I'll come back for my things when you and Mickey aren't here." She moved to the front door, opened it. "Mickey's been at the community center daycare several times. He knows some of the kids. He'll be all right there until the agency can send over someone new." She stared at Trace for a minute, her eyes as sad as he felt. Finally she shook her head. "Goodbye."

And then she was gone. Out of his life. Ready to be a memory. And he let her go, let her think he'd called for a replacement because he didn't have the guts to let an intelligent, beautiful, loving woman into his small little life.

The earth pitched and rolled off kilter, never to be righted again. Cold surrounded him. She'd taken all the warmth with her.

She prized her freedom. The one thing he couldn't give her. And he didn't have anything better to offer. Best for her to go now than after he'd allowed her to become his whole world.

He shook himself, heard Mickey's cries, and thought he was already screwing up.

Mickey's tears dried up when he saw Trace. He jumped up and down and grinned. Trace lifted him, his heart melting when Mickey laid his head on his shoulder.

Nikki had been right. Mickey's love and trust were unconditional, a gift Trace had never expected and vowed to treasure. "It's you and me now, kid."

He carried the baby into the living room and set him down next to the coffee table with a couple of plastic cars.

"Neeki?" Mickey asked, looking around, as if he understood something was wrong.

"Nikki bye-bye," Trace told him.

"Bye-bye work?" The kid wanted specifics.

Trace wouldn't lie to him. "No. Just bye-bye."

"No." Mickey shook his head wildly. "Neeki!" He toddled around the coffee table, grabbed Trace's hand and pulled. "Neeki."

Mickey wanted Trace to go after Nikki, to chase her down and bring her back. "You might actually have a chance with her. She loves you." Trace had no doubt about her feelings for Mickey. "I could probably have parlayed her affection for you into something, but I couldn't settle this time. Not this time."

"Daddy!" Mickey pulled on him. "Neeki."

"This is my fault not yours," Trace told him. "She's going to find someone who will love her…" The words trailed off as he replayed what she'd said in his head and realization dawned. The world slowly righted itself. "'*I'll find someone who will love me back.*' She loves me."

He picked up Mickey, swung him around and planted a big kiss on his mouth. "She loves me. Let's go bring her home."

Nikki brushed the wetness from her cheeks, angry with herself for the tears. She'd started the day with such hope, and now her heart ached, broken because she loved a man too damaged to risk being hurt again.

Well, it was his loss. She'd have given him her love and devotion, traded her independence for a family. She'd have been the best thing that had ever happened to him.

The vehicle in the next lane honked. She glanced over and saw it was Trace. For a moment joy swelled and filled her.

He'd followed her.

Then reality hit. He probably wanted her to honor her contract until a replacement could be found. She took pride in her reputation, but that was an assignment she couldn't accept.

Police lights flashed in her rearview mirror. He was pulling her over. She shook her head and pushed her foot down on the accelerator, defying his authority. He had no legitimate reason to stop her, and her battered heart couldn't take anything more today.

"Pull your vehicle to the side of the road and stop," his disembodied voice demanded.

"I don't think so." She continued to defy him, knowing it would end there. To pursue her any more blatantly would invite public notice and a rejection he wouldn't invite.

"Nikki, pull over now. I only called the agency to free you to accept the teaching job."

She blinked at his reflection in the rearview mirror. Determination stamped his features. He'd known about the offer? She saw heads turning in their direction as she passed the community center. Her hands tightened on the wheel as she turned on to Main.

She was safe. No way he'd expose himself in the middle of town. It would take more than mere affection for him to take such a step.

She deserved a man with the capacity to love as big as she did. Trace had proved he wasn't that man.

The Sheriff's vehicle pulled onto the street behind her, and her heart began to pound faster even as she cautioned herself against reading too much into it.

"Nikki Rhodes, I love you." Not only did he declare himself, he ramped up the volume. "Please stop."

Her throat constricted with emotion, love for him bursting through her in joy and euphoria. He loved her.

Wait. She breathed deep, forcing herself to slow down and to question if he'd really changed and could open himself to a loving relationship. But it was useless.

Trace loved her!

"Nikki." His voice boomed again. "Please pull over so I can ask you to be my wife and Mickey's mother."

"Yes," she whispered, as people turned on both sides of the street to observe their small parade. "Yes, please." Her hands shook as she pulled to the side of the road in front of What a Woman Wants. Women flowed from the shop to see what was going on.

Ignoring the rest of the world, she pushed open her door, ran to the man who held her heart and flung herself into his arms. Trace caught her—as she'd known he would—and swung her around, his head buried against her.

After a moment he lifted his eyes to meet hers. The love she saw shining in the emerald depths made her breath catch.

"You just announced yourself in front of the entire town."

"I love you, and I don't care who knows it." The words reinforced the pledge in his gaze. "I couldn't chance losing you." He set her on her feet and kissed her, his mouth on hers in the sweetest of promises.

"Neeki!" Mickey clapped his hands in the backseat of the SUV.

They looked from the baby to each other. Trace brushed the hair behind her ear. "Marry me. Be the mother of my children. What do you say? Let's give a dog a happy home?"

"Yes," she whispered for him alone, and then, loud enough for the world to hear, she repeated, "Yes!"

Pulling his head down to her, she kissed him, putting all her love into the embrace. Applause exploded around them, the perfect soundtrack for the perfect moment.

* * * * *

Aella closed her eyes and sensed a distinct shift, like movement from the world around her to the unseen world.

She opened her eyes. And had a slight shock at the man standing ten feet away. He wasn't just any man. Her heart leaped and pounded. He reminded her of a fierce warrior from an ancient civilization. Incan? She wasn't sure but she felt his deep power and masculinity.

I'm Aella. Are you the guardian of this sacred site? she asked, hoping her telepathy was strong.

Fox's entire body soared with joy. Fox struggled to put his personal pleasure aside.

Greetings, Aella. I'm the assistant guardian to this sacred area. You may call me Fox. How can I be of service to you, Aella? he asked.

I'm searching for a green sphere. A legend says that the Emperor Pachacuti had seven emerald spheres created for the Emerald Key necklace. He had seven of his priestesses and priests travel the world to hide these spheres from evil forces. It is said that when all seven spheres are found, restrung and worn, that Light will return to the Earth. The fourth sphere is here, at your sacred site. Are you aware of it? Aella held her breath. She loved looking at him, especially his sensual mouth. The desire to kiss him came out of nowhere.

Fox was stunned by the request. *I know of the Emerald Key necklace because I served the emperor at the time it was created. However, I did not realize that one of the spheres is here.*

Aella felt sad. Why? Every time she looked at Fox, her heart felt as if it would tear out of her chest. *May I stay in touch with you as I work with this site?* she asked.

Of course. Fox wanted nothing more than to be here with her. To absorb her ephemeral beauty and hear her speak once more.

Aella's spirit lifted. What *was* this strange connection between them? Her curiosity was strong, but she had more pressing matters. In the next few days, Aella knew her life would change forever. How, she had no idea....

*Look for REUNION
by USA TODAY bestselling author
Lindsay McKenna,
available April 2010,
only from Silhouette® Nocturne™.*

HARLEQUIN® *Romance®*

ROMANCE, RIVALRY
AND A FAMILY REUNITED

THE BRIDES
of
BELLA ROSA

William Valentine and his beloved wife, Lucia, live
a beautiful life together, but when his former love Rosa
and the secret family they had together resurface,
an instant rivalry is formed. Can these families
get through the past and come together as one?

*Step into the world of Bella Rosa
beginning this April with*

Beauty and the Reclusive Prince
by
RAYE MORGAN

Eight volumes to collect and treasure!

www.eHarlequin.com

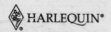

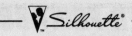

SPECIAL EDITION

INTRODUCING A BRAND-NEW MINISERIES
FROM *USA TODAY* BESTSELLING AUTHOR

KASEY MICHAELS

SECOND-CHANCE BRIDAL

At twenty-eight, widowed single mother
Elizabeth Carstairs thinks she's left love behind
forever....until she meets Will Hollingsbrook.
Her sons' new baseball coach is the handsomest
man she's ever seen—and the more time they
spend together, the more undeniable the
connection between them. But can Elizabeth
leave the past behind and open her heart to
a second chance at love?

FIND OUT IN

SUDDENLY A BRIDE

*Available in April
wherever books are sold.*

LARGER-PRINT BOOKS!

GET 2 FREE LARGER-PRINT NOVELS PLUS
2 FREE GIFTS!

HARLEQUIN® *Romance*

From the Heart, For the Heart

HRLP10

HARLEQUIN *Presents*

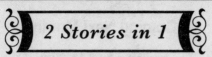

2 Stories in 1

HER MEDITERRANEAN PLAYBOY

Sexy and dangerous—he wants you in his bed!

The sky is blue, the azure sea is crashing
against the golden sand and the sun is hot.

The conditions are perfect for
a scorching Mediterranean seduction
from two irresistible untamed playboys!

Indulge your senses with these two delicious stories

A MISTRESS AT THE ITALIAN'S COMMAND
by *Melanie Milburne*

ITALIAN BOSS, HOUSEKEEPER MISTRESS
by *Kate Hewitt*

Available April 2010 from Harlequin Presents!

www.eHarlequin.com

HP12910

HARLEQUIN Romance®

Coming Next Month

Available April 13, 2010